THE SEARCH FOR REALITY

EVELYN GRIMALD

TARNEY BRAE CREATIVE ENDEAVOURS

*This book is dedicated to those who have suffered and
survived.*

1

———

"**W**hy are we here?" Marc Rushing asked. Well, it was more of a whine, but the other man, the shorter and plumper and far more determined Charlie Wash, studiously ignored that fact. "You took one look at the people coming to audition and stormed out of there."

"I couldn't do it." Charlie shrugged, shoving his hands into the pockets of his waterproof jacket. It wasn't really raining, though, only a bit grey. Still, every native Londoner knew when the weather was indicating rain, and this was the day for it. Charlie raised his shoulders and grimaced at the pavement. "Every single one of them looked so fake, so cursed eager and ready to please. Half of those girls had barely any top on at all, for goodness' sakes. I just wanted a bit of class. Elegance."

"Those are the options, considering it's an acting post. In a film. Those were professional actresses who came to audition," Marc pointed out. "What did you expect?" He looked around for a place to get out of the street and talk some sense into Charlie. The other man pushed steadily ahead, brushing past the myriad of people who walked along the street.

"I *know* that," Charlie grumbled. "I just wish we could have cast the part with someone already established. At least that would be a known entity. At least then we would know that she could act. Instead, we get these inexperienced acting school monstrosities who would as soon throw themselves on top of us as actually read a line. Who want their big break in the world, their one shot at stardom. What rot."

"You're the one who wanted someone new, someone unheard of. You said, and I quote, 'we need someone that the world doesn't know, who just grounds the whole film'. Which is exactly what I put in the advert." Marc stopped in front of a brownstone building and rubbed his temple. He looked every bit the part of assistant to the director, tall, trim, with clothes that were both comfortable and stylish. "Look, Charlie. It's not as if we can just pluck someone off of the street, okay? Why don't we just go back, I can handle the initial audition and we'll go from there, okay?"

Charlie shuffled his feet on the sidewalk and worried at his lip, the sign that he was thinking. He froze, lifted his head and put on a grin that had Marc quaking in his top-of-the-line shoes. "You are an absolute genius."

"Oh, dear. What did I do this time?" As soon as Charlie got one of these ideas into his head, there was no stopping him. Marc knew this for absolute fact; he'd been working for Charlie for years. That was what made Charlie the best director out there. His money made him a producer, but people knew him for the films themselves. And these wild ideas made Charlie that much better than the rest. They gave Marc a headache most days, and dealing with the results had occasionally been the stuff of nightmares, but that didn't matter. Not when it came to Charlie Wash's vision.

"Pluck someone off the street." Charlie grinned like a schoolboy and even went so far as to give a little twirl. Some of the people walking past gave the pair a sideways look before hurrying on. "That's exactly what we'll do."

"You can't be serious. You want to take some unsuspecting girl out of her life and throw her into a film with some of the well-known names in movies, even in America, and expect everything to turn out alright? The world just doesn't work this way! This is, by far, the craziest idea you've yet had," Marc hissed, his eyes wide as he tried to impress onto the director just how insane the idea was. Charlie waved a plump hand dismissively.

"It was your idea," he practically purred.

Marc rubbed his temple again and wished that he hadn't said anything. Things were generally safer if he did that. He looked at the building they were leaning against and saw that it was a cafe. "You know what, let's go in here, have a nice cup of calming tea and a couple of scones and we'll talk this out. I'll deal with the auditions, I swear, if you'll just give up this notion of—"

"Not a chance, Marc," Charlie said, pulling open the door and marching into the cafe. "You're my assistant and that is exactly what you are going to do. Assist. Now, come on. I'm going to need some food if I have to hunt down a girl today." Marc cursed, hunched his shoulders and dutifully followed his boss. It looked as though it was going to be a very long day.

There was no one behind the counter and there were no other customers. The cafe would have appeared closed, were it not for the soft classical music coming through the speakers, the lights illuminating a classic and timeless décor and the multitude of pastries in the glass case. As the door closed behind Marc, a soft feminine voice called from the back, "I'll be with you in a moment."

Charlie took that as an unspoken blessing to peruse the pastries and exclaim over each one. Marc gladly seized on the food as a distraction from this ridiculous search for something that could never be. No sooner than had he decided on a cup of tea and the delicious-looking apple tart, then the person belonging to the voice came out and all Marc's hopes were dashed. She was beautiful, with a relatively slim figure with curves in the proper places; her hair was chestnut brown and put back in a bun, though strands had escaped their hold; she had softly coloured skin the gentle colour of fog before twilight. Most of all, though, was that her eyes were a deep blue and quietly sad. Without a single word from Charlie, apart from a gasp, Marc knew.

This woman, young and lovely, was going to be the leading lady in Charlie Wash's newest film. Heaven help her.

2

———

"I apologise for the delay, gentlemen," she said, setting down a glass serving tray full of iced biscuits. "These had just come out of the fridge and I was icing them."

"Oh, there's no need to apologise," Charlie managed, though he sounded a little dazed. The young woman smiled gently and smoothed her hands on the simple black apron that covered her dark trousers. She wore those and a simple dark green tunic sweater and somehow made both Charlie and Marc seem under-dressed. Neither of them could bring themselves to care.

"Is there something I can get you?" she stepped closer to the counter, allowing her name badge to flash in the weak sunlight streaming through the windows. Dove.

"Er," Charlie managed, looking to Marc in desperation. The dark-skinned assistant had enough presence of mind to nod and order.

"A pot of tea, I think. And some, uhm, scones?" He hadn't meant to make it sound like a question, but Dove didn't appear to mind. She just pulled out some plates and picked up a couple of blueberry scones with tongs, setting them out.

"Would you like some jam with that? I have strawberry and orange marmalade. I can also warm those up for you, if you like." Marc shook his head and Charlie followed suit. Dove nodded and punched in a few numbers into her register. "Alright, then. That'll be seven pounds twenty three. And I'll get started on your tea."

In a daze, Charlie and Marc sat at one of the small tables, their scones in front of them. "I know what you're going to say," Marc warned, but it was too late. Charlie had the idiot's grin on his face that made it perfectly clear to Marc that his boss was set in stone. He had to say it, though, for the sake of being able to say 'I told you so' after things went pear shaped. "You can't just pluck her out of her life here and expect that she'll work out. I mean, can she even act? And what about her job here?"

"If she agrees to it, then there's no problem. That's what contracts are for, after all." Charlie took a bite of his scone and looked at Marc with triumph. "See," he said around a mouthful of crumbs. "Even you can't argue with that."

Marc turned his attention to his own scone and

hoped that this woman had more sense than Charlie. She came out a moment later with a pot of tea and two mugs, setting everything out before the two men and folding her serving tray under her arm. "Is there anything else you need?" Dove asked.

"Actually," Charlie said, swallowing hastily. "I wanted to ask you something."

Dove responded with a practised smile that said, quite clearly, 'I'm flattered, but not interested'. She waited politely for him to ask, though.

"Have you ever considered acting?" Charlie asked once he had managed to sip at his tea. Dove furrowed her brows, confused. This was certainly not what she had been expecting. She looked at Marc and he shrugged, indicating clearly that Charlie was being serious. Dove put the serving tray on the counter behind her and gave a shrug of her own, this one far less cavalier.

"Not really," she said. "Excepting my foray into theatre during school, that is. And the fantasy of every young girl to be a film star. Do you work for a theatre company?"

Charlie scoffed in pleased derision at the question. "A theatre company? No, no, my dear. I direct films. I've just started a new project, actually. I'm out scouring for new talent."

Dove laughed, shaking her head in disbelief. She gave Charlie a wry smile with a hint of darkness behind the look. "I suppose that means you want me to be in your film?"

"Would you?" Charlie grinned, practically bouncing in his seat. Dove frowned and shook her head, not quite sure how to take the man seriously. Who did he think he was, coming into her cafe and spouting such nonsense? She'd heard far more believable lines from far less savoury characters. She took a step away and put her polite smile back on.

"I'm sorry." Dove raised her hands to put a distance between her and Charlie. "I have my work here to occupy me. If you gentlemen need something, please don't hesitate to ask." She hoped that was the end of it, that she could now go back to her kitchens and continue working, but she hadn't counted on the determination of the supposed director sitting in her cafe.

"I understand that this is a strange conversation, that you probably don't want to hear this, but I am perfectly serious," Charlie said, reaching out as if to grab her wrist. "I don't know how else to say it. I want you in my movie. Tell me what I have to do to make this happen."

"How do I even know that you are who you say you are?" Dove challenged, her voice as gentle as ever, though her gaze held suspicion. "You could have been simply passing by and thought you'd play a prank on me. It wouldn't be the first time."

"He is who he says he is," Marc assured her. "Charles Wash, director and producer." He pulled out his phone and searched for a profile of his boss on a well-known news site. The picture came up and Marc handed his phone to Dove. She examined it, comparing person to picture, before sighing and returning Marc's phone. "And he is perfectly serious about the offer."

"You know nothing about me," Dove protested. "And, besides, I have my work here that I can't just abandon."

Charlie leaned back in his chair to admire the cafe. "Is this yours? It's very charming. Not a lot of independent cafes still floating around the city."

"I inherited it from my father," Dove said. She pointed to one of the corners, where a few wingback chairs were gathered around a low coffee table. "He used to sit there every Thursday evening with the neighbourhood elders, playing poker. They had quite the game going, until he died."

"I'm sorry for your loss." Charlie smiled sympathetically. Dove shrugged and wiped her hands on her apron.

"It was a long time coming," she said matter-of-factly. And she didn't particularly care to talk about it. "He had cancer. I took over this place about six months ago."

"Have you always wanted to run a cafe?" Marc asked. He pulled a chair over from another table, gesturing to it with what he probably hoped was a friendly smile. It simply looked a bit desperate to her, though not in an unkind way. Dove looked around at the otherwise empty cafe and resigned herself to a longer conversation. Obviously these two men weren't going to leave her be until they had it out. So she sat and crossed her legs, resting her hands in her lap.

"I've always been good in the kitchen," Dove admitted, "but I went to university to read philosophy. This place is about the closest I've come. You don't have to look so upset. It was Dad's wish that I do something practical with my life. He was always determined that I make money, and philosophy, well, that wasn't quite what he had in mind. But the cafe lets me talk with interesting people, and I've a steady income. That's more than most these days."

"So you don't actually want to run the cafe?" It was basically the same question, but with a sharper barb. Dove rubbed her thumb over the back of her hand and cast her deep gaze on her shoes. There was a pregnant pause which neither Charlie nor Marc could reasonably think about breaking. Dove wondered if they knew what they were doing, asking her to deny her father's dream for her and admit to only a mild liking for her work. Why did they have to come into her cafe? Why couldn't they have left well enough alone?

"No," she said finally. "But that doesn't mean I'm going to up and run off to be in a movie. This is what my dad wanted for me, and I'm doing well. I bring in a decent salary and I'm not dependent on anyone else for my living."

"Except the ghost of your father," Charlie pointed out. Dove's throat tightened for a moment, and she was sure her distress showed on her face for a brief moment, as Charlie gave her a sympathetic smile.

"Please, Dove, just hear me out. I'm offering you a chance to get away from the cafe for a while. Not permanently."

"If I leave, how do you expect me to return?" Dove asked, her tone slightly bitter. She twined her fingers together, trying to remain calm.

"We'll pay you for however much it would take to run the cafe in your absence, on top of whatever profits you could expect," Charlie said definitively. Dove blinked and her lips straightened into a thin line. "Would it be possible to get someone in to run things while you're gone?"

"You're acting as though this is as real as me stopping by the shops to get my evening meal." Dove looked closer at the two men, noting their high-end clothing as well as the way they seemed to view the world. "You seem to think that everything is within your grasp, as though you can just buy me!"

"I'm sorry if we're giving you that impression." Charlie put on a bit of a pout and a regretful look. They were likely affected, if this man was truly a director who worked with actors all day. But they seemed genuine. Dove was not unaffected by the apologetic look he gave her and her gaze softened into the sad smile she usually wore. "I would never want you to think that you're for sale. Look, Dove, the whole reason that I wanted you for this part was because of two things."

"What?" Dove asked, as though she were slightly afraid to know what it was. Charlie waited until she lifted her gaze to his and pointed, one at a time, to her eyes.

"Those sad, lonely blue eyes," he said. She raised her eyebrows at such a cheesy statement and Charlie laughed. "It's true! I don't want you because you can be bought. I want you because you'd be perfect for the role. And I'm really running out of ways to try and flatter you into this."

Marc cut in at this point, filling in where his boss had floundered. "This is not some sort of whim. Charlie is perfectly serious, including his reasons for wanting you. I have no flattery to add, but I will say that having money is better than not. No, wait, please don't be offended. I just mean that we're not trying to buy you, but nor are we underestimating you. And I'm not making this any better, am I?"

"Not particularly," Dove said. "Though I understand what you're trying to say." She turned her head towards the windows and watched the people walking past. "You treat this so lightly. This is my life we're talking about. These things don't just happen."

"We understand that, truly," Charlie nodded firmly. Dove glanced at him and shook her head minutely. "Look, Dove, how old are you?"

"Twenty-three," she answered quietly. "I graduated from university and started working here six months ago. Seven, almost."

"And you have already admitted that you don't want to do this for the rest of your life. That this wasn't your dream, right?" Charlie leaned forwards, putting an arm outstretched on the table, making certain that she knew his entire attention was focused on her. He looked determined, as if this really was real life, not some ridiculous fantasy that normal people could never experience. As if this was, indeed, true.

"Yes," Dove breathed, nodding. *The despair in her voice did not match the expression on her face and suddenly, neither Charlie nor Marc doubted that this woman could act. There was something in her manner, something more than her father dying of cancer and leaving her with the cafe. About that, she was merely resigned. This was more. She was actually scared. Of change or of something else?*

"You're young, and if you'll pardon me, gorgeous. Don't settle for less than what would make you happy. I can't promise you philosophy, but I can promise you a change of pace, something new, a chance to take life by the head and go with it," Charlie enthused. Dove bit her bottom lip and took in a deep breath.

She looked around the cafe again, her eyes resting on the chairs in the corner as if she were seeing a group of men sitting there over cards, grousing about their lives. She let the breath out slowly and said, "'If someone offers you an amazing opportunity, but you are not sure you can do it, say yes—then learn how to do it later.'"

"Who was that, Aristotle?" Charlie asked, *using all of his skill gained with actors to hide the smile that was about to break out onto his face.* Dove didn't miss the expression, though. She just replied with a smile that did not quite reach her eyes.

"Richard Branson," she replied. Charlie and Marc didn't catch the joke for a heartbeat, then they looked at each other and started laughing. A moment later and Dove joined in, her quieter sounds more musical than the full-bellied guffaws of the two men.

"Does that mean you'll give it a shot?" Charlie asked once the laughter had settled. Dove nodded.

"There are a few conditions," she said, "but I'll do it."

"Conditions?" Marc asked, pulling out his phone to take down notes. Dove blinked and tucked a strand of hair behind her ear, suddenly more hesitant than before. Marc threw her a reassuring smile. "Go on."

"Um, well, you said you would pay the amount that the cafe would take to run?" Dove asked, unsure of whether she should press whatever luck had wandered through the door. Charlie, on the other hand, just waved his hand and Marc jotted it down.

"That and profits. Of course, you can keep it open, if you want. Just get someone else to run it while you're gone. Take a leave of absence, that sort of thing," Charlie said. "Your cafe will be taken care of."

"Oh, right," Dove said. "Thank you. I, er, know someone I could ask about running things. It would take me a couple of days to train her, but... I think she'll say yes."

"So, you can come in on Wednesday, then? I would give you the week, but I had hoped to begin filming next Monday," Charlie said. "I have everything else sorted out but you."

"Wednesday should work," Dove murmured.

"What other conditions did you have?" Marc asked. Dove frowned and shook her head.

"No, that was it. Just making certain the cafe is taken care of," she said. Both men stared at her unbelieving and suddenly Dove felt terrified. Excited—she could at least admit that to herself—but terrified. She laughed nervously. "I feel as though I'm walking into this completely unprepared. I don't even know what this film is about! Or what part you want me to play."

"We didn't tell you?" Charlie widened his eyes and grabbed Dove's hand in apology. "So sorry about that. It's going to be a lovely little romantic drama about this woman—that will be you—who falls in love with an older man and her psychologist. It's a meeting of two generations and the journey to repair a damaged soul. Trust me, Dove darling, you're absolutely perfect for the part."

Dove grew slightly pale. "You want me to play the lead?"

Charlie shrugged, "Well, yes. I would have thought that was obvious. Oh, please don't back out. I know you can do it. We'll take care of everything, all you have to do is memorise a few lines, act and go to the premier. It's that simple."

"I've determined to do this, so I will," Dove said firmly. She pressed a hand to her stomach to hold back her nerves. "I never expected this when I came in to work today. I'm not normally this jumpy."

"Jumpy? Darling, you're charming," Charlie patted her other hand. Dove merely shook her head. Marc opened his mouth to say something when the door opened and a troupe of people came in, hoping for an early luncheon. With an apologetic glance, Dove stood and moved to go help her customers. Charlie grabbed her wrist and Dove froze, eyes wide. He released her and fixed her in a dazzling grin. "Wednesday, right?"

"Yes," Dove nodded. She pulled out a pad of paper from her apron and scrawled down some information. "This is my telephone number and my e-mail. Just send me the details and I'll be there."

"You won't back out?" Marc said. Dove shook her head.

"My word is my bond," she said quietly and slipped off through the people to take care of her business. She hardly had time to think about what she had done for another twenty minutes. And even then, the conversation and noise in the little cafe were hardly conducive to thinking. All she could do was watch in stunned silence as the two men finished their tea and left, looking pleased. Her entire life was changing right in front of her eyes, all for no reason at all but one man's whim and the fact that she had sad eyes.

Dove leaned back against the counter and shook her head. Sad eyes. A fact that wasn't her fault, nor was it something she seemed able to control. And here it was, changing her life. She had never wanted to be a film star. She had only wanted to bury herself in the dusty tomes of the university library and try to unravel the minds of the greatest thinkers in history. She wanted to understand people and the world and... Dove pushed herself away from the counter and went to go clean tables. There was no point in mourning what was, she told herself. It was time to look forwards. If they were serious, then she would embrace the opportunity with open arms. If not, then it was another one of those strange interactions she could talk about later.

The rest of the day went fairly typically for a Sunday. People came in a relatively steady stream from luncheon until just before supper. Then, as it was a Sunday, Dove pulled the blinds down and locked the door, closing so that she could go home to enjoy her own meal. She had managed to successfully avoid thinking about the potential consequences of her actions. All she had thought was that perhaps it was time for her to get out of this cafe. She didn't love it. That much had been clear from the moment she had been informed of her father's wishes. Now, she had a chance to go and try something new.

"Oh, who am I kidding," Dove sighed as she put the leftover pastries in a box to take home to her neighbours. "I have no idea what I'm doing."

She pulled out her phone and searched through the contacts until she found the number she wanted. Hitting the call button, Dove held the phone to her ear and hoped Meg picked up. "Hello, Meg Jones," a chirpy feminine voice said.

"Meg," Dove said, "It's Dove."

"Dove Graves! My goodness, love, what are you doing to be calling so late? Why aren't you preparing your baking for tomorrow?" Meg demanded. Dove sat in one of her chairs and leaned back.

"Frankly, because I need your help," Dove said quietly. She closed her eyes. "Are you still trying to get out of that waitressing job over on Fifth?"

"You have no idea. I need to make more money, to support Timothy, now that he's going to school, but my manager won't give me more hours." Meg started a rant and Dove found a faint smile. Nothing changed with Meg.

"Well, I have a proposition for you," Dove said. "How would you like to take over the cafe for me? I need to take a leave of absence and you were the first person I thought of to manage--"

"A leave of absence? Honey, is there something wrong? Oh, something hasn't happened to Peter, has it?" Meg gasped, referring to Dove's long-absent brother.

"No, of course not. He's still off in... Thailand, I think? No, I was offered a sort of new-job-type-thing, but I don't want to give the cafe up," Dove hoped that she could get away with not explaining everything that had happened to her that day. Meg wasn't going to take no for an answer, though.

"How about this? I'll stop by and, as long as you

don't mind Timmy hanging around for a bit, you can tell me everything that's happened and get me trained up. All those years of cooking for my family are not going to go to waste," Meg said. Without another word, she rang off and Dove was left wondering what had just happened. She realised, after a moment, that Meg had agreed to take on the cafe and that there was no possible way that Dove was going to get out of relaying her new job.

Dove's own astonishment at the events of the day was nothing compared to what Meg thought. The woman, staring openly with her hands poised on her rounded hips, let Dove get as far as, "I think I'm going to be in the next Charlie Wash movie?" before letting out a cry of glee. Meg grabbed Dove's arms and danced her around the cafe, leaving Timmy laughing and clapping his six-year-old hands and wanting to get into the fun. Dove let Meg take a turn with her son, wrapping her own arms around her waist and worrying her bottom lip.

"Charlie Wash?" Meg said when she finally stopped dancing around. Timmy was clutching her leg and laughing the breathless laugh of a happy child. Meg's own brown eyes were bright and she had a distinct cheer in her coffee-coloured skin. "Dove, do you even have any idea who Charlie Wash is?"

Dove shook her head. "I haven't had much time for films lately. Not after everything with, well, you know. And you know how terrible I am with actor and director names. Now, authors or philosophers and—"

"I know, I know, you can recognise it in an instant," Meg rolled her eyes, though she was smiling. "Love, Wash has done everything from psychological thrillers to sappy romance to high-fire action. He's huge in the movie world and there's not a movie of his that I've seen that I don't like. Except that one horror movie." Meg shuddered and Dove laughed.

"Was that one of his? The only movie I've seen in the last three years and it was terrible," Dove said.

"Well, I'd never seen horror before. Neither had you, for that matter," Meg sighed. "And we'll never do it again." Dove nodded in agreement before slumping into a chair.

"Meg, what am I getting myself into?" she asked softly, eyes wide and scared. "I don't know anything about acting in a film. The last time I did any acting at all, I was playing Irene Adler in a bad adaptation of Sherlock Holmes. That was ages ago!"

"If I recall correctly, you were a fantastic Irene Adler. Besides, how hard can it be? They'll be there to guide you and you just have to unravel the human condition. Think about it like philosophy or psychology. Just imagine what it would be like to be in this person's shoes? Who is she and how does she represent humanity? It's just a mental exercise."

Dove considered and nodded. "You're right," she said. "It's just a different mental exercise. I've done loads before. Oh, gosh, I hope I'm not terrible."

"You won't be," Meg stated. "Only you, Dove, would be more worried about the acting bit than the meeting famous people bit. Do you know who else is going to be in the movie?"

"We just talked about this," Dove said. "I don't know actors or directors. And Mr. Wash never mentioned anything about anyone else."

"He probably didn't want to frighten you," Meg said. "Not that you would know, but still, it's the thought that counts. As soon as you find out, I want to know." Dove replied with a weak smile. Somehow, this conversation wasn't actually making her feel any better. She stood and started to the back.

"Come on, Meg, let me show you where the recipes are. Then we'll deal with the orders from the wholesaler and I think we can call it a night," Dove said. Meg set Timmy in the chair Dove had vacated and put his Nintendo gaming device in his hand. Saying nothing more about Dove's new life, they got to work.

That didn't stop Dove from feeling a knot of nerves in the pit of her stomach.

3

———————

Wednesday came both too soon and not soon enough. All the time that Dove was awake, be it training Meg—who took to her new position with great alacrity—or running through the books for the cafe, there was a weight in Dove's stomach. She didn't know if it was fear or thrill, and she doubted that she would find out until she showed up on Wednesday. That was when she actually convinced herself that all of this was real, and not some elaborate joke. After all, movies and directors didn't just fall from the sky and beg you to take a leading role. That was fantasy, not reality. Those thoughts didn't help her waking fears, much. And when Dove was asleep, her dreams became startling enough to make her toss and turn, often waking her in the middle of the night.

So when Wednesday dawned bright and early and Dove stood in front of her window, watching the light, she met the day with relief. The baker's hours that the cafe had forced her to keep, and the pressure of anxiety, made certain that Dove was fed, showered and dressed by six. Since Charlie's e-mail message—surely that was confirmation that this *wasn't* a joke—had said she would be expected around eight, all Dove could do to deal with her nerves was stop by the cafe on her way.

Meg was already dealing with the early morning customers, smiling at the men and women who shuffled into their offices before the sun had really risen. They ordered things for take-away and seemed to regard the world through bleary, half-awake eyes. It was Dove's favourite part of the day, when she didn't quite dislike the cafe enough to want to close early and escape. She had expected that watching it from the other side would have given her a sense of longing or nostalgia, but all it gave was a quiet smile. No, she did not love the cafe, despite her father's hopes and wishes.

Dove slipped behind the counter during a quick lull in the lines and Meg beamed. "Dove! I wasn't expecting to see you today. I promise I followed all of the instructions and haven't made a mess of things."

"I'm not worried about it," Dove said frankly. "There was a reason I offered you the job, after all."

"Well, naturally, I thought it was because of my stunning good looks and the fact that you can't keep your eyes to yourself whenever I bring Timmy by," Meg laughed and pulled out a paper mug for the older man in a suit who was wearing a frown that could curdle the milk in his coffee. One of the regulars, Dove recognised. And just as surly as ever.

"Yes," Dove admitted once Meg was done punching the order into the register. "I'm very keen on Timmy."

"Everyone is," Meg said. She filled the cup and handed it over with a pleasant smile and a 'have a nice day'. The man huffed and walked out the door. Meg shrugged, as she had done for the last two days, and got on with things. Dove watched how easily Meg had picked things up and hoped that her own new life worked out just as well. She was never so easy with change as Meg, though.

Meg tilted her head and looked at Dove, her brow furrowed with concern. "So, not to push, but why are you here? You want me to make you a cup of something? Or are you having second thoughts? "

"I'm always having second thoughts, but I gave my word and I will see it through. Well, at least until they figure out I can't act and send me on my way. I'll grab some things," Dove said, "but I can get it. You tend the customers and I'll just take the owner's cut." She moved behind the counter and pulled together a simple cup of tea and a box of pastries. Worrying her lip, Dove hoped that the pastries would do much to soothe the tension over the figure she had come up with for the running of the cafe. If her acting didn't throw Charlie off, she was certain this might. She didn't want to seem as though she were taking advantage, after all.

Dove sipped at her tea and leaned against the

counter, suddenly quite worried. She cast her eyes on Meg and blurted the first thing that came to mind, "Do you think I look alright?"

Meg raised her eyebrow and put a hand on her hip. She looked over Dove critically and the younger woman practically quaked under Meg's gaze. "You look stunning. I mean, I know you were probably going for professional, but honey, you look stunning. There's a reason why black is so classic."

Dove had chosen tailored black trousers and a light black sweater, not quite certain how she should dress. Business attire seemed a bit much for an acting post, but neither could she be casual. She tugged at the slight gold chain at her throat. The pendant was a gold feather no larger than her pinky nail and was about the only jewellery she owned. She had put her hair back, but there were always a few strands that escaped and curled around her face. "I hope it's not too, well, dramatic."

"You're going into acting," Meg pointed out. "Drama is your business, now. So pick up your tea and pastries and go to work. Okay? Trust me, you'll be just fine."

Dove smiled weakly. She dutifully picked up the pastry box and tea and walked towards the door. "Meg, thank you so much for doing this. I, well, just thanks."

"Don't mention it, honey. And don't worry. You are going to go in there and take them by storm."

Dove smiled again, stronger this time. She gave a wave and left. Meg was right. She could do this. She had done much the same with everything else in her life, be it philosophy or the running of the cafe. She was just scared because she had no idea what to expect. Or if she even should expect anything at all. Yet Charlie, Marc and Meg thought she could do this. So she would.

With straighter posture, Dove left the cafe without a second glance and walked the rest of the way to where her new life would begin.

The place where she was meeting Charlie and Marc was a large warehouse. It looked less decrepit than the others around it, but that was only because all of the windows were intact and there were a number of cars sprinkled around outside of it. Despite the early hour, there were already people moving around, carrying things, directing people, going from one place to another. Dove didn't even get noticed when she stopped a woman carrying an armload of costumes and asked for directions to Charlie Wash's office. The woman jerked her head, not impolitely, towards the inside of the warehouse.

"Third door on the right. It's got a plaque, you can't miss it," the woman said before moving off. Dove nodded and walked inside, depositing her empty cup in the recycling bin as she did so. She clutched the box of pastries closer to her and adjusted the cross-body bag she wore. Then she stepped inside the warehouse and entered a different world.

The intact windows and cars aside, the exterior gave absolutely no indication of what was held within.

The warehouse had been converted into a fully finished building with electrical lights and dry walled rooms that looked like offices. The centre area was still generally open, with various pieces of lighting and camera equipment strewn about. It looked like a thriving business, not some thrown-together affair. Dove wondered vaguely just how much money was going into this venture. Her mouth went a little dry.

She counted three doors in and, indeed, saw the plaque. Relief spread through her and she stood straighter, swallowing the urge to run. Dove raised her hand to knock and was interrupted by the door opening. Instead of Marc or Charlie, a man stepped out, slipped past Dove as though he was an expert at getting around people. "Sorry," he gave her a distracted look and shook his head. "I need a drink. Care to help?"

Dove doubted that was an invitation, more of a plea to point him in the direction of something strong. His meeting must not have gone well. "I don't know about a bar or pub being open this early, but there's a little Irish bakery two blocks away. They'll add a bit of whisky to your coffee if you ask nicely."

The man smiled charmingly. "You know, that sounds perfect. Thanks." With a wave, he was off. Dove was left standing in stunned silence, her eyes wide. He was just about the most handsome man she thought she had ever seen. And she had seen all types coming through the shop. He was probably forty—a full seventeen years older than her!—but Dove couldn't seem to bring herself to care. At least, it wasn't a terribly strong argument against admiring his physique as he walked away. He was of a decent height, with broad shoulders and fit form, sculptured features, tousled dusty-brown hair and eyes of light green that could sell your soul. Her encounter had only lasted a few seconds, but she already couldn't get his image out of her mind.

Some people crossed in front of her line of vision, startling Dove and making her remember the reason why she was there. She blinked and forced her thoughts back to what she was doing. She knocked on the office door and hoped that whoever that man was, that he would be around in the future, if for nothing else than to distract Dove from her fear. Her silent hopes were cut short when Marc opened the door, looking frazzled for all that it was barely eight in the morning. At the sight of her, he visibly brightened.

"Dove! Oh, you're here!" Marc stepped aside and ushered Dove into the office. It was fairly small, there being only limited space in the warehouse. There was a single round table in the room with four chairs perched around it. Charlie sat in one spot, fiddling with a pen and some paper and Marc's spot was indicated by the presence of a stack of papers and a computer. The other two spots were only significant in that they were empty. "Look, she came!" Marc gestured grandly.

Charlie shot out of his chair and practically ran to Dove, grabbing her face and kissing each cheek with a vehemence that was certainly not European. "You have no idea how glad I am to see you," Charlie preened. "I think you're the only thing that's gone right today."

Dove held out her box as the only response she could think of. "I brought pastries," she said softly, trying to smile. Charlie stared in wonder and beamed up at Dove, laughing boisterously.

"That's it, you are officially a miracle worker," he thundered. Marc took the box and Charlie held the chair for Dove. She sat and the two men sat in their respective chairs. "I think this is going to be a wonderful relationship. I can already tell that you are going to be a hit with everybody. Not to mention Wes. Let's get all of these details hashed out so that I can go and show you off."

"Um, okay?" Dove said, not entirely sure what had just happened. And who was Wes? She dug through her bag and pulled out the papers she had painstakingly prepared, handing them over to Marc and Charlie.

"What's this? More conditions?" Charlie laughed. Dove shook her head while Marc perused the paper.

"No. I went through the books for the cafe going back two years. I tallied up the total profits for the cafe, taking into account the cost of running the cafe. Ordering supplies, employee time and so forth. I then took a basic projection of what the profits would be in the future based on current profits and past profits. The last piece is the cost of hiring a full-time employee, as well as all of the benefits that are included therein. That number at the bottom of the second sheet is, er, my price," Dove said. She felt slightly awkward about asking for such a sum, especially considering how much money had obviously already gone into the production. She was not going to back down, though. If they wanted her to act in this movie, then that was what they would have to pay.

She was certain that, at least, she wanted them to accept. It wasn't a hoax, and she was surprised to find she was actually looking forwards to acting. To trying something new. To escaping the cafe and living her life how she chose to live.

Marc pointed to the figure at the bottom of the page and Charlie glanced at it before laughing. Dove frowned. They weren't going to pay her? Fine. Then she would take her pastries and go. She reached for the open box when Charlie scrawled out a number on his pad of paper and turned it to face Dove. She froze, furrowing her brows. "I don't understand," she said after a moment of silence.

"That is what we will pay you," Charlie said. Dove looked at the number again and merely felt more confused. The number was far larger than anything she had come up with, and she had spent half of Tuesday running numbers. In fact, it was about five times her original figure. "On top of the cost of running your cafe."

Now, she was just astonished. "I can't take that," Dove breathed, shaking her head. "That's far too much!"

Now it was the turn of Charlie to be confused.

Marc merely kept a straight face and put Dove's paper on top of his stack. "What do you mean?" Charlie asked. "Did you think that I wouldn't pay you for what you're doing?"

"No," Dove stated. "No, this is too much like trying to buy my affections."

"What am I going to have to do to convince you that I'm not trying to buy you?" Charlie threw his hands up and leaned back in his chair, obviously not in the mood for getting into another argument. He looked at Dove, completely serious. "Dove, darling, please believe me. I truly believe that you're worth that amount. If only I could get you to believe that, too, then things would be better."

The barb stung. Dove was willing to admit that much. To insinuate she didn't value herself? Sure, she had some days where it was difficult not to believe that working in the cafe was all she was worth, despite her dreams. Everyone had those days, didn't they? But that a near stranger seemed to value her more than she herself did, that hurt a little. Wordlessly, Dove sighed and nodded, giving her assent. She didn't much feel like arguing the point, either. And the money would go a long ways towards making her life anew. She would just have to get over the guilt of taking the money.

"Good," Charlie said. Marc handed Dove a contract and a pen, smiling as though she were entering into something good. Dove, on the other hand, was just thinking how much she didn't know about what she was doing. Still, she had given her word and agreed to being payed. It was a very large amount of money, and Charlie seemed convinced that she could do it. That, more than any of the rest, made her agree. She would sign the contract. After glancing through the pages for anything unsuspecting. It all seemed fairly straightforward, though there was the stipulation that she be on call until after the premiere for whatever, but she could live with that. Dove signed her name in her precise hand. She handed the contract and the pen back to Marc.

"Thank you, Dove," Marc said. "You don't know how much this... just, thank you."

Dove replied with a smile. She tried to make it genuine, but there was something niggling in the back of her mind that said she failed. Miserably. So much for acting.

Charlie stood and grabbed her hand, pulling her out of the chair. "Don't be scared, darling. You are going to be fantastic. I saw your natural talent the moment I laid eyes on you."

"As long as you tell me what I'm meant to be doing," Dove murmured. Charlie chuckled and threaded his arm through hers, leading her out of his office. Marc, ever the dutiful assistant, trailed behind.

"Oh, you'll get tired of me doing that very quickly, I assure you. Now, how about a tour? This warehouse has been under construction for the longest time. I think we've finally got it up to snuff in regards to a movie set. We have all the rooms built up for the internal shots that we'll need—except for a pub, which we'll rent out. Or build, if I can't find one I like.. Oh, and Wes' flat. Not his actual flat, the one in the film. The external shots are going to be done as the weather permits. See, we need rain. But look! Here's where a good portion of the film is going to be done." Charlie gestured to a room that looked completely out of place.

It was a sort of office setting, complete with floor-to-ceiling bookshelves and leather chair, but there was also a longer couch and desk. The styling was from the 1940s with some modern touches, such as a computer. It was a whole composed of incongruous pieces, but it looked both intelligent and comforting. Exactly what a psychologist's office should be.

"Um, Mr. Wash," Dove said.

"Ugh, what a terrible thing. Charlie. I am always Charlie." He shook his head and his round face fell into an expression of obvious disdain. Dove laughed quietly.

"Charlie, then," she said, a hint of a smile at the corner of her mouth. Just hearing him talk and point out his domain was setting her nerves to rest. "I don't have a script."

Charlie blinked in astonishment, eyes wide and mouth dropping open a little. He pulled Dove away from the office room and dragged her along. "Darling, why didn't you say so in the first place!" he exclaimed. "I want you to have a good look at this script, okay? There's a cast meeting tonight and we'll make introductions and so forth. But have a look over the script."

Dove nodded. Charlie brought their rapid parade

to a stop outside of a cramped room where three people were sitting around a single desk, each with a computer or pen and paper, all talking at and over each other. At Charlie's entrance, one of the women stood and rushed over to him. "Charlie, thank goodness," she said. "The boys and I can't figure out how to finish off that one scene in the pub that you wanted us to rework. We're thinking and thinking and there—"

"We'll discuss this later," Charlie said, his voice full of authority. It was more serious and demanding than Dove had ever heard from him. The woman backed down, giving absolutely no doubt that his order would be obeyed. This must be Charlie's director voice, the one that commanded authority and was responsible for such a successful reputation. Dove hoped that she would never have occasion to feel the quiet fount of power that bubbled beneath Charlie's normally amiable surface.

In another moment, the stern demeanour was gone and Charlie was back to smiling widely. "We need to get a script for our dear leading lady here. Dove, I want you to meet the geniuses behind most of what is going to be put into the film. This is the best writer team I've ever worked with, so I just keep taking them with me from movie to movie. Annie, Ray and Jose."

Annie bobbed her head in what might generally be termed a polite nod. She snapped her fingers and Jose materialised at her side, a script in his strong hand. Dove took the collection of papers with a grateful smile. She and Charlie backed away, and the writers immediately took to ignoring them.

"They seem dedicated," Dove said. "Not terribly conversational, though."

"Oh, well, they just don't like actors. It's all a question of interpretation, I'm afraid. Unfortunately for both actors and writers, it's what I want that matters most." Charlie shrugged, smiling broadly. He paused in front of another collection of people doing their best to argue their way through a stack of plywood. "Okay, darling. Go study that script. Your dressing room—yes, you have your own—is all the way in the back of the warehouse and up a flight of stairs. It'll be the first door you see, okay? Meet back in the main space at five. Ta!"

He waved her off and Dove was left clutching the script, absolutely dazed. This was unlike just about anything she had ever done. Whether or not that was a good thing was an entirely different question, one she was still considering. She took a deep breath and glanced down at the title of the script. *Closing the Distance.* Dove tucked a strand of hair behind her ear and shook her head. "This is going to take some getting used to."

She went off to find her dressing room and study the script. Or maybe text Meg and see how the cafe was doing.

4

———

The coffee helped. The added bite from the Irish whisky finished what the coffee started. By the time Wes downed the dregs of the bitter drink, he was feeling far more amiable towards the world.

He sat in the farthest, darkest, most secluded corner he could find in the coffee shop and started down at his empty cup. Weston Blackwood. One of the most well-known names in the movie industry, working in both British and American film. He had been selected for various magazine awards for Most Eligible Bachelor and Sexiest Man. He was worth an enormous amount of money. And here he was, working on a romantic drama.

"Damn you, Wash," he growled, leaning back in his chair. Just because he owed the man a favour wasn't any reason why he should put up with such nonsense.

Him? A strictly romantic movie? He hadn't done such trash since the early days of his career.

What was worse, he snarled mentally, was that they wanted to pair him off with some girl nearly half his age. A contrast of young and old, making something beautiful out of a stigma common in society. Okay, sure, he wasn't opposed to a pretty face, no matter the age, but there was something fundamentally wrong with him being set with a practical infant, maturity-wise. He was thirty-seven, for goodness' sake. He hadn't even met the girl, yet, either. What he *had* done was read the script; there were scenes in there he wouldn't have wanted to do with an actress he hadn't known for a while. Knowing Wash, they would be tasteful and essential, but still. Wes had his standards. There was no way that he was going to do those things with someone he had never met, not to mention a relative baby.

He had tried to explain his objections to Wash that morning, but the man hadn't been at all interested, claiming he was righting a societal wrong, working for women's rights and art and people's rights to love whoever they wanted to love. Wes owed him a favour and had signed a contract. That was that. So he had practically fled the scene. Thank goodness for tech assistants who lived around here.

"Is there anything else I can get for you?" The girl was perhaps still in school, working a job to earn extra spending money. But the way that she had her uniform shirt unbuttoned perilously low and the way she stood with her hip cocked gave the impression that she was trying to be much older. The way she stared at his face only solidified the fact. Whatever calm the alcohol had given Wes vanished and he curled his lip in disgust.

"No," he said, standing up and pushing past her as if she wasn't even there. He shrugged into his light jacket and left the cafe. Wes sure as hell didn't want to be set upon by women at the moment. Women were currently his problem. Well, young women.

He supposed he shouldn't be surprised that girls wanted to practically jump him. He was in the best shape of his life—thanks to a personal trainer—and wasn't lacking on the looks side, either. It wasn't arrogance, he knew, it was simple fact. It was, after all, part of the reason why he was doing so well in the movie industry. He just wished that he could meet someone who cared about more than that. Not some child who was convinced of her own self-worth and probably more interested in what he could do for her than him as a person.

Well, Wes frowned, where had that come from? He wasn't looking for a relationship at all! Was he?

Before his thoughts could spiral down into more depressing ideas, he came upon the warehouse again. The movie set that was going to be the place where he practically lived for the next ten months to a year. It certainly didn't look like much on the outside, but the inside was done in typical Wash style. Which is to say done to the point of excess. Wes didn't want to do this film, but that didn't mean he didn't like Wash. Actually, the two were good friends, most of the time. The problem came when Wash cashed in that favour that Wes owed him from all those years ago. Accrued during the dark times of Wes' life.

"Good morning, Mr. Blackwood," one of the techies said. He thought he recognised this one, an older man with the look of someone possessive of his equipment. Wes remembered; the techie was a sound guy and had done more than a few of Wash's movies. Damned if Wes could remember the man's name, though.

"Morning," he said in reply, offering a smile in return. It was as fake as could be, but most people couldn't tell the difference. Some days, Wes couldn't even tell the difference. He kept the smile on his features as he trudged up the back stairs to his dressing room. It was, he knew, the only sanctuary a body could find during filming. He outfitted his room accordingly.

The door was closed behind him before Wes allowed his pleasant demeanour to fall. He stared at the room before him and sighed. It was fairly small, but larger than some spaces he had dealt with. There was space for a couch that was wider than normal; it was a good place to sleep. There was a vanity that he could convert into a desk or table, a chair to one side. The colours were dark and soothing and there was a cupboard, and area for a tea kettle. Wes knocked his shoes off and put his phone on bluetooth, scrolling through his music for something that fit his mood. He settled on Charles Brown.

Then, he collapsed onto the couch with a blanket

on his feet. Wes stared at the ceiling and let the music sweep him away. Before too very long, he was asleep, the frown on his features smoothing away.

It seemed like seconds later when someone came pounding on his door. Wes sighed and looked up. He had been sleeping on and off during the day, even taking time to glance over the script again so he didn't look the fool at the cast meeting that evening. Now, someone was disturbing his solitude and he found he wasn't terribly pleased.

"What?" Wes called through the door. He fiddled with his phone, contemplating whether or not he wanted to start a conversation with any of the people in his contacts list. No, he would much rather be left alone to wallow in his folly. The pounding on the door continued. "What?" Wes snarled again, this time standing and shuffling over to open the door. He found himself faced with Marc.

"Sorry, Wes," Marc said with a shrug. "Orders to fetch you to the meeting."

"What time is it?" Wes asked, finding it difficult to be angry at Marc. Wash, yes, but Marc was only doing his job.

"Five fifteen. Charlie wasn't happy when you didn't show up on time. He wants you to meet the new girl," Marc said. Wash stifled a yawn and nodded. He put his shoes back on and grabbed his copy of his script, shaking his head so that his bed-flattened hair looked somewhat normal again.

"Fine. Is there food there?" Wes asked, following

along behind Marc and trying his best to pull his polite persona out to the surface. It wouldn't do to offend everyone on the first day. Marc shot him a look. "Yes, right. It's Wash. There's always food. It's just that I haven't eaten anything today."

"Well, I don't know how much there is in the way of substantial food. I think there might be some sandwiches and salads and fruit. The usual fare," Marc said. "Sorry." Wes shrugged in acceptance and breezed into the conference room behind Marc, his eyes slightly lidded, his smile slight but present. It was his charming and handsome look—as described by several magazines and blogs—and it served as the best apology he could come up with.

"Wes! There you are." Wash threw up his hands and grinned broadly. He was standing with some of the other actors in the film. They were all people Wes recognised and he waved his hand slightly before slipping towards the buffet table.

The majority of the people had already come and grabbed their food. They were now standing around and talking with one another until Wash called the meeting to order. All except a slightly familiar girl with chestnut-coloured hair. Wes frowned for a moment before he recalled her. The tech crew woman from that morning. He wondered why she was here. Usually, this was an actors only—except for the heads of departments—meeting. She was looking over a selection of sandwiches and, judging by her expression, considered it a trying task. It was her eyes, Wes decided, because she wore a pleasant smile. Her eyes were the deepest blue he had seen and carried the weight of the world. Sad eyes.

"There's not much selection, is there?" Wes stepped closer to her, curious to see what she would do. After all, that morning, she had directed him to a cafe rather than stare at him or ask for his autograph. He had ignored it at the time, but then, had been a bit preoccupied with Charles Wash and his great directorial vision. She glanced up at him and then back down to the table, the only change in her a slight shift of her weight.

"I'm having a hard time deciding between the turkey and Swiss and the chicken and artichoke panini," she said, pointing to the two different sandwiches. Wes considered, watching her reaction more than he looked at the food. She made none, just waited to see if he would give input. When he didn't, she grabbed the panini and excused herself with a smile. Wes shrugged and grabbed the turkey sandwich, glad there was someone in the world who was more impressed by a sandwich then by him. Well, not *glad* per se, but it was a novel feeling. Freeing, almost. He sat down in the vacant chair around the conference table that was meant for him and started in on the sandwich.

Since when did he over-analyse an interaction over a buffet table? This was what came of not eating things all day after being forced to do something you don't want to do, he decided.

Wash, seeing that everyone was present, gestured

towards the table and sat down. People filled into their respective seats. There was Rachel Whittington, a slightly heavy-set middle-aged woman who looked like she could be everyone's best friend. She and Wes had worked on several pieces before, and he considered her a very good actress. Then Roman Dawes, a man of about Wes' age with friendly, guy-next-door looks. He and Wes had been good friends for years, even if they occasionally competed for similar roles.

There were other actors and actresses there, meant to fill in the gaps. A few younger girls, as well. Wes examined them, wondering which was the one he was meant to be pairing against. The blonde woman at the far end of the table with hair that looked like it had come straight from an Instagram influencer, had the looks for it, but she didn't seem intelligent enough. Then there was the woman with glasses, whose gaze seemed to analyse everything, but she didn't seem the sort to star in a romance movie.

Wes didn't know. He tried not to care.

"Alright, alright, settle down," Wash called, waving his hands in an attempt to demand order. Everyone quieted, their attention turned to the director or the last pieces of their food. Wes saw the techie stuff the final corner of her sandwich into her mouth as she gave her attention to Wash. He shook his head. "Well, hello all! Welcome to the first official cast meeting of *Closing the Distance*. This is where we all introduce ourselves and go over the script. Voice any problems you have now, because after this meeting, I'm going to assume that you are fine with things. Right, introductions first, though. No, I don't care if you already know each other, there are new people here, so off we go."

Wash looked pointedly at Marc, who coughed and muttered out, "Marc Reynolds, Assistant to the director."

"You'll go to Marc to air out any grievances, okay? If he deems them worthy enough, he *might* bring them to me. Now, moving on," Wash said. He nodded and pointed to the next person. "Name and Character."

"Jenny Tolls," the blonde woman said with a happy wave. "I'm playing Hanna."

Hanna. Wes glanced over his script and saw that Hanna was the sister of the main female protagonist, Casey. He was pleased that this Jenny wasn't going to be his counterpart. It just didn't feel right. Rachel was playing the Sheriff and Roman was meant to be Wes' character's best friend. Wes was next and he dutifully looked around and smiled a winning smile. "Wes Blackwood. I'll be playing Vaughn Marshall, psychologist."

Jenny glanced at glasses—a Katie who, thankfully, was playing a bartender—and tittered something under her breath. Katie nodded and the two blushed profusely. Wes bit back a sigh and glanced pointedly at Wash. Then, he realised something. Jenny and Katie were the only two girls at the table young enough to be playing the part of Casey. Excepting—

The tech assistant was next and she gave a smile

that didn't quite reach her eyes. "I'm Dove Graves. I'm to play the part of Casey Wood."

The room seemed to vanish for the roaring in Wes' ears. *No. No. Flat out no.* That was the woman meant to be his counterpart? She looked nothing like an actress, not to mention that she… She what? Wes couldn't find a reason why it shouldn't be her, but there was something in the back of his head that told him no. Yet, once he had accepted the fact, there was no one else at that table that could possibly have been cast to play the part of Casey. Sad, distant, wearing a front that most people wouldn't look past. She was pretty, but not a supermodel. She had intelligence in her mien and that something else that was required of film stars. So why was Wes so shocked?

Only years of training kept Wes from showing his astonishment. He flashed a mild smile at Dove, who was looking at her script, a slight touch of red in her cheeks. The others at the table nodded and smiled. Wash took over the meeting again and the moment had passed. Wes focused his attention on the director and turned his mind from Dove. At least, he tried.

"So now that you know everyone, let's start in on this script. Any grievances to air?" Wash practically barked. Having worked with Wash before, Wes knew full well that you could air whatever grievances you wanted, but it wouldn't matter if Wash was bound and determined to have something in the film. Pretty much all of the time, such ideas worked out, but Wes knew of a few times when an idea that Wash was determined to keep had been cut out in final editing. Still, constructive criticism aside, Wes wasn't brave enough to air his grievances first. Especially not after the argument of that morning.

"Actually," Dove spoke up, flipping through a few pages. Wes turned to stare at her in shock. Of all the people to start off, she was not the one he had expected. Did she know how this world worked at all? "I was wondering about the beginning. The whole premise with Casey having escaped from a serial killer and walking into the police station with a bloody knife, well... isn't that a bit much?"

Wash frowned and considered. He read the scene in his own script, then folded his hands on the paper. "What would you suggest, darling? After all, that is the premise of Casey's psychological problems. The whole reason why she seeks Vaughn out to begin with."

"Yes," Dove agreed, nodding slightly. "But a serial killer seems a bit too fake. As a representation of reality, that just doesn't fit with the rest of the film. It's outlandish. Maybe you could have a violent rapist or destructive ex-boyfriend or a mugging gone wrong. Any one of those would be more believable."

"A serial killer isn't believable?" Wash asked in a deadpan voice. Dove either didn't see the deep waters she was heading into or she didn't care. Wes was impressed.

"They only seem to happen in movies," Dove said. "It isn't realistic or believable. And it throws this whole movie into the realm of unintelligent tropes that would never apply to real life."

"I see," Wash said. He frowned deeper and looked through the first scene again. He glanced at Marc to see the assistant's response and around the table at the various actors. Wes decided that it was his chance to speak up.

"I agree with Dove here," Wes said, leaning casually back into his chair. He maintained eye contact with Wash, who drew his brows together. After a moment, Wash nodded and scrawled something into the script.

"Very well. Mugging gone wrong, then," Wash said. "Still gets Casey where we need to be and lends a certain 'believability' to things."

"Thank you," Dove said quietly, writing something into her own script. Wes smirked to himself and shook his head. Young or not, aware of how the film industry worked or not, she was certainly interesting. Sad eyes. Fighting spirit. That did not mean that he wanted to do this with her. Maybe if she were ten years older, Wes wouldn't be so frustrated.

The rest of the meeting went fairly well, with a few minor critiques and changes made to the script. It was a fairly standard romance, with a few deeper musings on life thrown in; Casey was mugged, went to Vaughn for psychological assistance, and a deeper accord started between the two. Frankly, it was a little simple for Wash's usual pieces, but then, Wash could do just about anything he wanted and get away with it. Even a romantic drama.

Wes himself didn't say anything until they got to the scenes where Vaughn and Casey were meant to have sex. Wash was usually tasteful in such instances, but that didn't mean it wasn't fairly explicit what was happening. The thought of doing such things with Dove, no matter how pretty, was something Wes didn't want to dwell on. Again, to his surprise, though, Dove spoke first.

"Um, Charlie," she said, a faint blush rising to her cheeks. "Are these scenes really necessary?"

This time, Wes could see plainly that Wash wasn't going to give up. "These are the culmination between Vaughn and Casey. They're meant to show the connection between the two ages, the two minds, the two hearts. It's a beautiful thing and absolutely necessary to the story. Dove, darling, this isn't a romantic comedy. This is a drama. This is, as you stated before, what life is meant to be. And we're going to show it, in all its glory. As you have agreed."

Dove's blush had faded until she was quite pale. She nodded and looked down at her script, flipping to the next page. Wes raised his eyebrows at Wash and the director just shook his head. They continued on with the remainder of the script, finishing off the few scenes that were remaining. Wes ventured a few comments and everyone else added something. Dove, though, said nothing more.

They finished going through everything around

nine. By that time, everyone was tired and wanting something more substantial than the tidbits they had been provided. Wes stretched and felt his back crack. Roman stifled a yawn. Wash gestured to Marc, who stood. "Well done, all. The changes will be incorporated into a new script and I'll get that to you tomorrow morning. We'll do a full read through and fix any further issues. Be here on time, people. Thank you."

The entire room seemed to surge upwards as one. The actors left in groups, taking their scripts with them and talking over the project, as normal people would do. Deciding that he should at least attempt to do this properly, Wes turned to go greet his counterpart properly and saw that Dove was already slipping out of the room, her script held tightly at her side. He shrugged and gathered up his own material. Wash came and slapped Wes on the shoulder, an incredible feat considering the man was a good foot shorter than Wes. "I told you it wouldn't be that bad."

"She's a child. She's fifteen years younger than I am and--"

"Fourteen," Wash said. Wes blinked and turned to the shorter man.

"What?" He asked incredulously.

"She's twenty-three," Wash said with a shrug. "Graduated from university six months ago with a degree in philosophy."

"You have to be kidding me," Wes snarled. "She's a baby! I'm more than a decade older than she is. And you want us to practically have sex."

"No," Wash said, his voice dropping to a quiet murmur. "No, I don't want you to have movie sex, where nothing ever happens."

"Not a chance, Wash," Wes curled his lip in disgust. "I'm not doing a porno, I don't care how many favours I owe you."

Wash recoiled and stared at Wes, equally disgusted. "You honestly think I would ever *consider* going into that industry. No! I'm not doing that. Ever."

"Then what are you talking about?" Wes hissed.

"I want you to seduce her. Well, no, not seduce her, per se. Get to know her. Become her best friend. Date her, even." Wash shoved his hands into his pockets and looked frankly at Wes. He was perfectly serious, Wes realised. It was bad enough that Wes had to act out such things with her, now Wash wanted him to actually date her? To, what, enter into a fake relationship with her?

"Why?" Wes demanded. "For the press? We won't even get nosy reporters in here until filming is almost done. The interviews aren't until much later."

"Not for the press," Wash said. He faced Wes and lifted his chin, donning his director's authority and making sure that Wes knew it. A moment later and the authority dissipated for something more human. "Wes, you're my friend. One of the few true friends I have in this business. Or at all. Despite the fact that I dragged you into doing a romantic drama, you are my friend. And you know I wouldn't ask you to do this if I didn't have a good reason."

"Then give me the reason," Wes said. Sure, the two of them were friends, but Wash was asking him to date—fake or not—someone who was fourteen years younger than him. Acting aside, there were things that friends didn't ask you to do.

"Because I pulled her out of a cafe where she was languishing. She was being stifled by an inheritance she didn't want and couldn't get out of without a considerable amount of money and guilt. She doesn't know a thing about our world. She has no idea what to expect when I put her into that set and throw cameras at every conceivable angle. I want her to have someone she trusts, who knows this world better than anyone else here. Who is going to stand with her and help her out, make her feel better after a day of me yelling at her. I want that guilt to go away," Wash said. He looked at Wes with puppy dog eyes after he had finished his speech and the actor groaned in annoyance.

"If I didn't know any better, I'd say bullshit. Unfortunately, I know better," Wes growled. Of course Wash would have altruistic motives for wanting Wes to seduce Dove. It didn't change the situation except for giving Wash's motives purity. Wes ran his hands over his head and massaged his neck, racking his mind for a way to say no. "Damn it, Wash. Nothing untoward, okay? I won't go that far, but I'll do what I can."

"Thank you," Wash said. He patted Wes on the shoulder again, this time in gratitude, before heading towards the door. "Go get some food and some sleep. I'll see you in the morning."

"One of these days, Wash, your pure motives are going to get you into a whole heck of a lot of trouble," Wes said. Wash nodded.

"I know," Wash said, and left. A moment later and he poked his head back into the conference room, where Wes stood alone. "Oh, and I think she probably hasn't dated much, if at all." He vanished.

Wes gaped after his director for a moment before carefully walking to the door and closing it, leaving him in the conference room without anyone the wiser. He stepped back into the middle of the room and let out a roar of anger. In a swift move, he turned and put his fist into the wall. His personal trainer had drilled him in proper boxing technique, so he rolled with the punch and felt the impact shudder all the way into his shoulder. The wall gave a little, leaving a dent where Wes had struck it. He pulled back and seethed through his teeth.

The wall wasn't going to be enough, Wes decided. He grabbed his script from where it rested on the table and stalked out of the room, slamming the door behind him. Wes dropped the script in his dressing room and left the warehouse, calling a cab and giving the address for his flat on the other end of town. Twenty minutes later and he was home, kicking off his shoes and reaching for his MMA gloves.

The punching bag in the corner of his flat didn't stand a chance.

5

————

*B*right and early, as promised, Wes showed up at the warehouse. He was still pissed and he wanted to make certain there was no doubt of the fact. He wore dark clothes, dark glasses and a snarl that could curdle milk. Everyone who took one look at him got out of his way. Quickly.

Wes trudged his way into the warehouse and marched to the conference room, growling curses under his breath. How could he have been so foolish as to agree to this? He knew how; it all had to do with that stupid favour from years ago. Necessary at the time, but now he was paying for it in full. By the time he was done with this film, it was more than likely Wash would owe *him*. With that slightly more pleasant thought in mind, though it was hardly enough to soothe his frayed nerves, Wes shoved the door open and ran straight into the one person he did *not* want to see.

Dove let out a stifled cry as she stumbled backwards and dropped the box she was carrying. The lid flew open and pastries fell out, littering the carpet with crumbs and sugar. "Oh, no," she breathed, crouching down to recover what she could. She threw Wes a glance out of the corner of her eyes and he would have sworn he saw ire there. As if he was the one deserving of reproach.

"Watch where you're going," Wes said, spouting out the first thing that came to mind. Dove stiffened. She didn't look at him, merely continued on with her task.

"I do, and I did," she said smoothly, as if she were perfectly calm and was only commenting on the weather. Wes winced. He deserved that one. He had been rude. Not to mention the fact that he was supposed to be seducing her, even if it never went anywhere. He was off to a great start.

Wes crouched beside Dove and picked up a croissant from the floor. "Look, I'm sorry," he apologised, putting as much sincerity as he could into the words. "I... didn't sleep all that well last night."

"I see," Dove said, as bland as before. She gave up on trying to get the crumbs from the floor and stood. Wes stood with her and took her in as she threw the box into the rubbish bin. She wasn't wearing black as she had done the day before, but the effect was just as striking. Dove had her hair falling down her back in a thick braid. Paired with the dark jeans and grey-blue sweater she wore, it made her look almost aloof in her beauty. Wes would have said she looked older, but there was still that something in her expression that practically screamed youth. And, of course, there were her eyes. Still sad, but now they were filled with wariness as well.

"I can replace the pastries, if you want," Wes said after a moment. "I truly didn't—"

"It's fine." Dove shook her head and moved away from Wes to take her place at the table. "They were for all of you, anyways."

If her words had stung before, now they cut deeply. Wes wasn't thinking anything about his agreement with Wash at that moment. He was thinking about the fact that he had clearly done wrong and if he didn't fix it, then working with Dove for the next however long was going to be, well, difficult. "I really am sorry," Wes apologised again. "Come with me to that cafe a couple blocks away and you can tell me what it was that you got."

"Wrong cafe," Dove said, tucking a strand of hair behind her ear. "And really, it's fine. It was an accident. There's no need to get all worked up about it."

Wes sighed and sat down next to Dove, tossing his script casually on the table. She watched him as though he were a snake about to strike. It wasn't fear, just awareness. And he found he didn't like it at all. "I know," he said. "I still feel badly. Let me make it up to you somehow." Dove raised her eyebrows in question and Wes thought frantically. "Thai food. This evening. I'll order it for take away."

Dove watched him for a moment, her eyebrows

drawn together. Wes returned her gaze, trying to figure out what she was thinking. Those eyes were inscrutable, and her expression gave absolutely nothing away. Well, at the very least, she would certainly be able to act. The moment was broken when Roman walked in the door, looking thrilled to be awake at such an early hour. Dove turned her head and sighed, "If it makes you feel better."

Wes grinned and nodded firmly. "Perfect. I know this great place that delivers. Anything in particular you like?"

Dove shot him an exasperated look and shook her head, whether in negation or frustration, he couldn't tell. More people walked in and the moment for conversation was lost. Roman settled across from Wes with a wave and Rachel sat on Dove's other side. Everyone filled in the rest of the spots until only Marc and Wash were missing. Roman groaned and leaned back in his chair. "Why are we here this early if our benevolent director isn't going to be here?"

"Because your benevolent director is nice enough to bring food," Wash said as he walked in. Marc was trailing behind, two boxes stacked in his arms. Dove stiffened beside Wes and he noted that the boxes were of the same kind as the one she had pitched earlier. What were the chances that Wash and Dove would go to the same cafe? Especially considering it wasn't the one closest to the warehouse. Food for thought, coupled with a collection of just about every type of pastry and Wes was intrigued.

"You're a godsend," Roman beamed and snatched up a strudel, taking a bite. "I didn't have time to stop for breakfast."

"Thanks," Rachel chimed, grabbing her own breakfast sandwich. Wes took a bear claw, but only after Dove had taken a croissant. He watched her pick the fluffy pastry to pieces, each minuscule layer going into her mouth before she carefully pulled apart the next layer. Nerves? Or just not hungry? He didn't think she was the sort to starve herself for looks, as many in the industry did. He narrowed his eyes and took a bite of the bear claw. He didn't want to be so intrigued by her. For one, there was the matter of their age difference. For two, there was that idiotic deal with Wash—Wes was meant to be seducing her for her own comfort and peace of mind, not actually interested in her. Not to mention that he was fairly certain she didn't much like him. She certainly wasn't intimidated by his fame.

"Okay, now that everyone's here and well fed," Wash said, settling into his chair, "let's get the script sorted out. And then we're just going to go straight into a reading, okay?"

Marc started handing out the scripts and each person glanced through it. Dove frowned slightly and turned to Rachel. "Um, a reading?"

"Oh, that's right," Rachel smiled, her demeanour friendly and almost matronly. "You've never done this before. I got the story from Marc, about them plucking you up from that cafe. It will go over great with the press."

Dove smiled wanly.

Rachel nodded, and continued, "So a reading is just what it sounds like. We go through the script and read it out, trying out different character styles and just generally getting a feel for things. If something feels like it fits, then stick with it. Otherwise, play around. I've done a reading that was meant to be straight American accents and ended up being Irish for the rest of the film. Great fun. Just relax and you'll be fine, alright?"

Dove nodded and opened her script, her features set, if not calm. Marc started off by reading the setting and the set-up of the opening scene where Dove's character was meant to be walking to a police station, covered in blood and holding a knife. Rachel's character, a police detective, came in and it was discovered that Dove had nearly killed the person who had mugged her. There was some consoling and then the scene changed to the mugger being sentenced to a heavy prison sentence and Dove shaking with fear in the background.

The reading went on like that, shifting from Dove barely managing in her life to her being introduced to Wes' character, the psychologist. At every scene, Wash demanded people to do different characters. Rachel was too nice, Roman not nice enough, Jenny needed to be less understanding and Katie needed more gruff sympathy. Wes was alternately not giving off interested vibes or was too distant. Wash had Wes change accents four times, even going so far as to make him try

German for a few lines. The only person that didn't seem to need prodding to get into character was Dove.

She was quiet, but not shy. Terrified of going out after dark, but unafraid of meeting new people or trying things. She was unsure of herself, and yet gave off unspoken confidence. Above all, though, were her sad eyes. And those were no character trait that she put on.

They read through the meeting of Vaughn the psychologist and Casey the victim and even got to the point of Vaughn running into Casey at the bar where Katie worked before Wash put a stop to things. Frankly, Wes was relieved. No matter how hard he tried, none of his ideas about how to play Vaughn seemed to please the demanding director. Besides the fact was that he didn't want to get into the more physical pieces with Dove. Sure, reading from the script had been fine. Dove had played off of his characters with more tact than some of the seasoned actors he knew. She hadn't blushed unnecessarily when she stumbled over a word and she didn't seem to regard this as a silly exercise; Wes looked to Roman on that front. No, Dove was perfectly pleasant. But she was also distant.

Somehow, by snapping at her and making her drop her box of pastries, Wes had inadvertently alienated her. He had apologised, profusely. That seemed to serve only as a further insult. Or maybe Dove was just nervous, scared, even naturally aloof. He would need to actually talk to her to determine that. He wasn't sure he was ready for that step.

Wes gladly took the break, winding his way through the warehouse to his sanctuary. He closed the door of his dressing room behind him and put his hands to his head. He had done some difficult things during his time in the film industry, but this task seemed to be taxing him more than usual. Why? Perhaps it was because he actually seemed invested in the outcome. Not just as repayment to Wash, either.

Wes was about to turn on his music when he heard someone go into the room next door. Huh. He hadn't realised that there was another dressing room on the second floor. He thought it was only his—and by intelligent design, too. Turns out he wasn't alone.

"Hi, Meg," Dove's voice floated through the shared vent between the rooms and Wes immediately searched for cover, fearing he would be caught. He relaxed and sat on the sofa. She couldn't possibly know he was here. "I didn't call at a bad time, did I?... Oh, that's good. There's usually a lull between the morning and lunch rushes... Mmm. Sure. The order forms are in the red binder in the office... Yes, that's the one... I'm glad things have been going well, there. I knew you were the right person for the job."

Wes was at a total loss. What was she talking about? Some sort of restaurant? No, wait, Wash had mentioned that Dove had come from a cafe or some such. Then Meg must have been the person who was currently running the place for Dove. Satisfied with his logic, Wes settled back to try and pick up any other nuggets of information that might be useful.

"That's great. I'm glad to hear it. Oh, the film?" Dove paused, as if considering her words and Wes straightened his shoulders. "We're doing a reading of the script today. Yeah, it's... No, the story is fine. Why would you say I'm not happy? Oh. Well, it's a big adjustment. I read philosophy in university and then I ran the cafe. I haven't done theatre since my schoolgirl days... That's kind of you to say, Meg, but frankly I don't care how much 'raw talent' the director saw. He's obviously functioning in a delusional state... If you want to call it a joke, then do so. No, it's not that... I just don't know. Maybe this is everyone else's dream, but it was never mine. I'm an amateur and all these people are... What has that got to do with anything? He can be charming, but that doesn't mean... Just leave it be, Meg."

Dove practically snapped the last bit and even Wes widened his eyes at her tone. She didn't seem quite capable enough of such vehemence or bite. Whoever Meg was, she was probably feeling that sting. "I'm sorry, Meg. It's, well, it's just I don't trust people terribly easily and I'd rather not place my trust in these people. As far as I can tell, they're flighty and expect the world to fall at their feet... No, I haven't seen any fans drooling around, but that doesn't... Fine. I'll reserve judgement until I've been here a week. It doesn't matter in any case. I've signed a contract and I won't break it. Just, well, keep doing what you're doing. You can hire extra help if you need it. I really do appreciate it, Meg. Yeah, you, too. Bye."

Wes waited until Dove had left her dressing room —the break was only fifteen minutes long—before he let out a long, low whistle. That conversation both explained much and very little. She didn't quite like him or his sort and she didn't feel as though she belonged. There were more questions than answers, he thought, but at least he had two things he could deal with. Luckily, both could be solved by the same means. Thai food would be a start.

Wes left the dressing room and went back down to the conference room, where the others were picking over the catered lunch. It was little more than some food from Tesco, but there was a salad and some crisps. Wes took his food to where Dove sat at the table and dropped into his chair with a sigh of relief.

"No matter that we're just doing some readings, I feel as though I've been running a marathon," Wes commented, going straight for the crisps. Dove carefully peeled an orange and raised her eyebrows at him. Wes shrugged. "Alright, fine, so running a marathon is much more difficult."

"Have you actually run a marathon?" Dove asked skeptically. Wes blinked, surprised more that she was asking a question than at the question itself. He nodded and stuck a crisp into his mouth.

"Yes," he said. "I have. There was a film I was in, oh, ten years ago that was about this man who went searching for himself by training for and running in a marathon. I did all the actual training and the running.

Nearly drove me crazy, but I was in really good shape by the end."

"I commend you for that." Dove shook her head. "I hate running."

"I do, too," Wes admitted. "Unfortunately, it does work. Nowadays, I tend to do a more general routine. There's not much marathon running involved."

Dove chuckled silently and shook her head, eating a section of orange. Wes continued eating his own lunch, hoping that her mild interest would spark further conversation. Instead, they both sat in silence, Dove seemingly content with eating and not talking and Wes trying to think of something to say. Finally, he threw his plastic fork into the salad container and looked at Dove.

"What?" she asked, sounding wary. Wes noted also that she moved away a fraction of an inch.

"Okay, I don't mean to sound arrogant, but have you actually seen any of my movies? This isn't for my own pleasure or to stroke my ego, but I'm trying to figure you out. And you don't seem to care at all that I'm a famous film star." Wes winced at the way his words sounded, but it was too late to take them back. To his pleasure, Dove didn't look offended or as frustrated as she had sounded when on the phone with Meg. That conversation was a large part of why he was asking.

Dove pulled a strand of hair out of her eyes and leaned her elbows on the table. "To answer your first question, no, I don't think I've seen any of your movies.

I never had much opportunity to see them growing up and during university, I didn't have the time. Now, I get along without. And as to your second question, no, I don't care that you're a famous film star."

"Why?" Wes asked. "Most people seem to be intimidated or try their hardest to seem nonchalant. You, though, truly don't seem to care." Dove turned her head resting on her hands to look Wes full on. She fixed him in her gaze and watched him for a moment more than he would have expected from someone ready to dismiss him as an arrogant actor.

"We all bleed," was all Dove said before turning her gaze away and pulling her script towards her. End of conversation.

Wes had the sudden urge to be elsewhere, so he stood and took his salad container to the bin. He lingered next to Roman, who was scarfing down the last of his sandwich. "What do you think so far?" Wes asked, not wanting to discuss the feeling that Dove's words had brought about. Both awe and fear and the knowledge that this person, nearly half his age, had managed a wiser attitude about life than he had, through all his struggles. Roman, on the other hand, was nothing like that.

"Well, for one, I never thought I'd ever see you doing a straight romance again," Roman said with a wicked grin. "What did Charlie have to do to get you to agree to this? Sell his soul?"

"My agent thought it was a good idea," Wes lied. Actually, his agent *was* pleased. Mostly. "She thought that it would be good to get me in every popular genre. Romance is popular so I get better publicity for my next movie. At least, I think it was something along those lines. What about you? I thought you were lined up for the next comedy out of Vancouver."

"Something fell through with the contract. They decided to get someone who could just fake a British accent rather than brining in the real thing." Roman shrugged, but Wes knew the man would rather be working on a comedy than romantic drama. Still, it was a Charles Wash film and ought to gross well.

"That is the way things work, after all," Wes said. "We are at the mercy of the contracts and the demands of the people. Still, maybe it'll be a nice change of pace. The script is interesting so far, right?"

"It is for you," Roman agreed. "You get to have the deep character who thinks about how people think. And you get to pair up with dear Dove over there. All I get is some supportive moments and a few exchanged glances with what's her name playing Hanna. Jenny, right? It's not a terrible role, but it's not Vaughn."

"Sorry," Wes said, meaning it. Roman was a good person and could easily pull off fairly complex characters. Because of his handsome, friendly looks, though, he played second fiddle more than he would like. "You could always get into television. There's a fair bit of money in that and the characters get to have more story."

"I've thought about it." Roman nodded. "Maybe I'll start poking around. Well, we have to get back to things. Our director has returned. Oh, and Wes? Stop looking as if you'd rather be somewhere else and enjoy the fact that you're acting next to a beautiful woman. And an intelligent one at that." Roman clapped Wes on the shoulder and went to sit down. Wes sighed and shook his head. He slipped back into the seat beside Dove, who was glancing over the rest of the script.

Wash smiled at the actors as though he hadn't seen them for days. Someone had a good lunch. "I hope you feel better after that. Because we're going to be here until we're done and your performance this morning was pitiful. I want to see energy and intensity. Got it? Good. Now, where did we leave off?"

Wes took a deep breath and settled in for another long session.

6

---

*D*ove felt completely out of her element. There was nothing about pretending to be someone else that felt familiar to her. Well, not in a situation so extreme as this, at least. She was good at thinking about the nature of the world, and she was good at running a cafe. She only loved one of those. And somehow, she was here, in a conference room full of professional actors who were capable of moving fluidly from one character type to another, with no indication of what was real. All Dove could do was hope that not too much of her own life slipped through into Casey's character.

"I can't do this anymore," Dove read, doing her best to put the appropriate amount of anger and desperation into the words. It was more difficult than she had expected, acting. Trying to feel what someone else was feeling. Trying not to let her own despair show through. She was certain her attempts were passable, at best. Then, at least no one was laughing at her attempts. "I don't know what I expected in coming here, but it wasn't this."

"Case, Casey," Wes read, this time acting Vaughn with a slightly brusker London accent. "Wait! You can't just run away from this and expect it to fix things."

"Why not?" Dove asked, demanding an answer. "Isn't that what you're doing, Vaughn? Running away from this? From us? And you won't even give me a decent reason as to *why*—"

"Not quite, Dove, darling," Charlie said, waving his hand to cut her off. She closed her mouth and waited. "No, you have to have more *despair*. This is the moment when you decide to walk away from the love of your life because you've realised he can't be everything that you want. I need you to think on the worst pain you've felt and channel that into your character. Okay? Good, now try again. From 'I can't'."

Dove didn't want to think about the worst pain she had ever felt, but at Charlie's words, it sprang immediately to mind, filling her thoughts and emotions like an insidious parasite. Her breath caught and Dove was barely able to think, let alone focus. She forced herself to focus, though, because she had done it before and she knew how to do so. Experience did not make it any easier.

"I can't do this anymore." This time, her voice was little more than a whisper, and she choked on the last word. She took a deep breath and forced herself to think. "I don't know what I expected in coming here, but it wasn't this."

Wes was a competent actor, Dove acknowledged through her haze, as he acted off of her pain. "Case," he breathed, "Casey. Wait." He paused and flicked his eyes to Dove, making the pain that much worse. She didn't need anyone looking at her right then. It would only make things unbearable. "You can't just run away from this and expect it to fix things?"

"Why not?" she spat, her fear at being approached putting anger into her voice. She pushed away at the memories and tried to separate what was her pain and what was Casey's. "Isn't that what you're doing, Vaughn? Running away from this? From us? And you won't even give me a decent reason as to why you don't think I'm good enough for you."

"It's not that I think you're not good enough, Casey," Wes growled, voice taking on a darker tone. "There's no one better. It's that I'm not good enough for you." In tune with his character or just acting out of instinct, Wes reached out to brush Dove's cheek. That was the one thing she couldn't take at that moment.

Completely forgetting about Casey and the acting, Dove shot straight up from her chair, eyes wide and gasping. "I, er, need to use the loo," she managed to stammer out before shoving away from the table and darting out of the room as fast as she could move. She dived into the restroom and locked the door behind her, sinking to the floor and pulling her knees to her chest. She struggled to contain her breathing, because if she didn't, she knew full well that she would launch into a full-blown panic attack.

Why, of all the possible times to have done such a thing, did Wes have to try and reach out and touch her face right then? When she was struggling to push her pain and fear aside. When the mere thought of human contact made her throat contract and her heart beat erratically. It reminded her of too many things and there was too much horror to contain. Which was why she was currently sitting on the floor of the restroom, shaking in terror. Dove let out a quiet moan and buried her head in her knees.

Someone started knocking on the door. It was a gentle sound, but still insistent. "Dove?" It was Wes. Why did he have to come? Why couldn't Charlie, or better yet, Rachel? "Dove are you alright?"

"I... I think I've got food poisoning," Dove said, thinking of the first thing that would keep her from having to leave the safety of that room. "Just—just give me a minute."

Indeed, Dove was beginning to feel physically ill. She pushed the feeling aside, knowing from experience that giving in would only bring on more issues. She closed her eyes and pulled her knees tighter to her chest, taking deep breaths. One, and in. Two, let it out. After thirty seconds, her heart had stopped racing and the terror that had come over her had dissipated. She was okay. Dove stood and splashed some water on her face, drying it and staring at herself in the mirror. She had looked better, she supposed, but she had also looked worse.

Dove opened the door and found Wes standing there, looking concerned. For a moment, Dove expected her heart to start pounding again, but it didn't. The moment had passed and she could go back to how things were between them. As long as he didn't push too deep into her problems, things would be fine. Just fine.

"Are you sure you're alright?" Wes asked, furrowing his brow and frowning over her. "You look pale."

"Just food poisoning. It hits me sometimes like that," Dove lied, the words as smooth on her tongue as the lines she had been reading. Wes' frown deepened, but he said nothing. Dove led the way back to the conference room and sat in her chair, ignoring the stares of the other people with the practised ease of someone who had done so before. "Food poisoning," Dove explained to Charlie. He glanced at Wes, who nodded and the director's shoulders slumped in relief.

"Well, we'll have to find a different caterer, then," Charlie said. Marc hurriedly scribbled something into the notepad he always carried and the reading went on. It was as if nothing had happened. They moved on from the scene where Dove had left and, much to her relief, she didn't have another episode. Nor was she scolded for not having enough grief or pain. Charlie prodded at her later, when she was supposed to be acting the love-sick fool over Wes. Wes was having the same difficulties, though, so she didn't take it too seriously.

Perhaps Dove would be comfortable enough to manage such scenes with time. It wasn't that he was older than her, though in the script that was much of it. It was because every time she tried to imagine something like that happening, she felt shy and frightened. Nowhere near the level of earlier, but still the fact remained: Dove wasn't any good at pretending to be in love.

The group made it through the end of the script more or less intact. Everyone was obviously tired and the constant pushing and changing of character had taken its toll on even the hardiest actor. Dove was practically slumping in her chair. She still felt a little wobbly after her near-attack earlier, but frankly, everyone else looked worse. Rachel was trying to be cheerful, talking about her dinner plans and finding a temporary flat for the duration of filming. Jenny listened half-heartedly and Roman was sitting with his head resting on his fist, eyes lidded. Even Wes looked rather the worse for wear.

"Well done," Charlie said, though the words didn't quite sound sincere. "It was a fair start. I want you to try and nail down those things we talked about. Get those scripts memorised. Tomorrow you all are meeting with costume and makeup, not to mention lighting and sound. I want to get started filming on Monday, so you had better be prepared. Got it?" There was a general murmur of acknowledgement throughout the room. Charlie waved his hand dismissively and Marc stood.

"Go get something to eat and a good night's sleep," the assistant advised. This was taken as a dismissal. People stood and started to leave, Dove among them. She felt bone weary and wanted to crawl onto her couch with a decent glass of wine and some take-away pizza. Wes stepped up to her.

"So, do you want to have a sit down meal or just get something for take-away? The Thai place isn't that far away, a few blocks, maybe," he said. Dove frowned, lost. She blinked and remembered the incident that morning with the pastries. She had agreed to allow Wes to get her some Thai food. Dove had hoped that he would just forget about it and was frankly surprised he had remembered.

"This isn't really necessary," Dove said. Maybe he would give up and she could have a nice night at home. "I'm sure you're tired, too."

"It's going to get a whole lot worse," Wes said. "The more you can power through it, the better it is. Which is why Roman and Rachel are going to go out and keep active. How about we just go and sit and let someone else serve us, okay?"

Dove nodded absently. "It gets worse?" she asked, following Wes out of the warehouse and hoping that he was just joking. She was surprised to find that it was dark out when they emerged from the warehouse. Had reading through the script really taken them that long?

"Oh, yeah. If it weren't Wash, I wouldn't be so

certain, but I've worked with him before. This was just a taster. He likes early days and long nights. I've worked on films where he has us doing the same scene over and over for nearly two weeks. And even then, we had to redo it later on. I suggest investing in some caffeine." Dove paled slightly at the description and hunched her shoulders slightly.

"I... didn't realise," she said softly. Wes chuckled sympathetically and put his hands in his pockets, the motion somehow making him seem more relaxed and casual than he had before.

"Right, all of this is new to you. I forgot that Wash pulled you out of a cafe. It was a cafe, wasn't it?" Wes said, glancing over at Dove. She nodded. "This must be a completely different lifestyle from what you're used to."

"Long days and hard work? Actually, it sounds about normal," Dove sighed. "It's just what I'm working on that's different. Acting isn't really my thing."

"You seem quite capable." Wes pointed to a small restaurant with neon lights in the window. "This is the place."

He held the door for Dove and she ducked in. The smells assailed her before she could register the sights and her stomach rumbled. The wobbly feeling of earlier vanished completely, reminding Dove that she hadn't eaten much that day. Picking at a croissant and an orange didn't count. The two were seated in an out-of-the-way corner and menus were handed over with a disinterested look from the older man who was running the floor.

"So, what's your poison?" Wes asked in his best American drawl. Dove looked up from the menu, startled.

"I beg your pardon?" she asked, not sure whether to be offended or frightened. Wes just grinned and held his menu up.

"Drink. What do you think about a drink?" he asked. Dove quickly averted her eyes from his handsome and charming smile and focused her attention on the drinks menu. The last thing she needed right then was to be distracted. At least she wasn't panicking anymore.

"I, er, think I'll just get some tea," she murmured. Wes raised his eyebrows and Dove shifted in her chair, feeling as though her every move were being scrutinised. Coupled with her exhaustion and the incident of that afternoon, and she was feeling very vulnerable. He, on the other hand, was looking very sexy. Dove mentally shouted at herself. Sexy? Where had *that* come from? Certainly it had nothing to do with the fact that his smile could stop traffic or that his eyes actually looked at a person when she spoke. Definitely not with the fact that a few strands of hair dangled into his face. A flash of memory coupled with imagination made Dove wonder what it would be like to have him touch her. Just like that, her thoughts shut down and that same shudder of fear slipped up her back.

"That sounds refreshing," Wes said calmly. Dove

was fairly certain that he had noticed her sudden stiffening, but he pretended otherwise. Of course, with him being a professional actor, it was difficult to tell whether he was being honest or was just hiding his reactions. "I'll get a pot and we'll share."

She nodded. Wes ordered from the older man, who said nothing and melted away into the recesses of the restaurant. Dove payed close attention to her menu to keep her thoughts from straying in a dangerous direction. She debated silently over the noodle bowl or the curry and decided that the curry was probably the best for keeping her awake. If what Wes said about the long days and hard work was true, she would need the help. Not that long days or work were unfamiliar to her.

"So, are you feeling recovered from your food poisoning earlier?" Wes asked, tossing his menu aside and looked at Dove as though she were the most interesting thing in the room. She shrugged and flipped through her menu to have someplace to look apart from his piercing gaze.

"It was fairly mild. I hadn't eaten too much," Dove said. She decided firmly on the curry and set her own menu aside. It was time to push cowardice away. She was here with Wes Blackwood and she needed to at least be cordial. Anything to the contrary would just make working with him more than difficult.

"I'm glad you're feeling better," Wes said. The old man returned with their tea and silently took their orders, vanishing as soon as Wes stopped speaking. The actor eyed the spot where their server had stood a moment before. "I think he does that just to scare people."

"It's certainly disconcerting," Dove agreed. She took a sip of her tea to hide the fact that she had no idea what else to say to the man. Their worlds were completely different. It wasn't as though she could ask him about his work—she was supposed to know who this famous actor was. And launching into a conversation about her own work would be rude. Thank goodness he seemed to know how to hold a conversation.

Wes leaned forwards slightly in his chair to show his interest in her answer, "So what is running a cafe like?"

Dove blinked. "What?" she asked, translating her question silently as 'why would he care'.

"Running a cafe," Wes repeated. "It's one of those things that is around in people's everyday life. I've never thought about what running one would be like. I'm curious, is all."

"It's not as charming as most people think," Dove laughed flatly. "I get people who come in all the time and exclaim over the pastries or the coffee and think that it would be such fun to bake for people every day and make such pretty creations. And talking to all the people."

"I take it things aren't actually like that."

"Not in the slightest," Dove said. "Terrible hours—waking up at four to get the things baking on time, or to take deliveries from the other bakeries around, then getting home around nine because you have to clean up and prepare for the next day's food. The people aren't nearly as pleasant, either. It's demanding a drink or food and complaining terribly when something is wrong. If there's any conversation besides, then they give small talk about the weather, hoping that you'll move quicker because you like them. I'm a good cook and a fair baker, but... it wasn't my dream."

"Is acting your dream?" Wes asked. Dove looked at him incredulously and he grinned. "I didn't think so."

"Honestly, I think I was just trying to make it through university with my mind whole," Dove sighed. "I never figured that I would be doing what I wanted afterwards, so I never hoped for anything."

This time, Wes was the silent one. His eyes widened and Dove winced. Why had she said such a thing? The last thing that anyone wanted was to hear her depressing life story over dinner. A friendly dinner to make up for spilled food. She wished that she could take it back and merely told banal stories over the tea. Unfortunately for her, she wasn't built that way.

"You never... everyone wanted to do something," Wes defended. "Even I wanted to do something. Come on, what did you want to be when you were a child? Didn't they make you draw pictures of that in primary school?"

"That was ages ago," Dove defended. "Things have changed since then."

"So? A great many children play at what they end up doing when they grow up. Or have some idea of where they're going. What did Dove Graves want to do as a child?"

"Travel," Dove said into her tea cup. It was the simplest explanation, she supposed, for that overwhelming desire to be anywhere other than where she was. As a child, it had occupied all of her thoughts. She had spent so much time over atlases, travel guides, researching dream vacations and exotic locations.

"Travel? Seriously?" Wes asked. Dove frowned.

"Yes," she said. "What's wrong with wanting to travel?"

"Nothing," Wes replied, holding up his hands in defence. "It's just that's what I wanted to do."

"Oh," Dove murmured. She was saved from having to embarrass herself further by the arrival of their food. For a moment, both people just ate and enjoyed the sensation of food after a long day. Then, feeling the need to apologise for snapping, Dove said, "I imagine you get to travel a great deal with your work. Or are all the places people go in films just green screen?"

"Some are." Wes nodded. "But there is travelling involved. I've been places that are meant to be some of the best spots to visit. And ended up spending the entire time working. It's not quite the same thing as going and experiencing a culture."

"At least you got to go," Dove pointed out. Wes nodded.

"Yes," he said. "There is that. I wouldn't give that up for the world. Sometimes, though, you just need to get away from things. Leave life behind and go somewhere where no one knows you."

You have no idea, Dove thought. "Where no one knows you? From what my friend Meg says, you're famous enough that such places are few and far between. Surely that has to be, well, an experience."

Wes pointed his fork at Dove, looking like one of her old professors about to scold her. Granted, he was far more attractive and considerably younger than they had been. The image remained, though. "That's the problem with you," Wes said. "I can't figure you if you're saying 'experience' as though it would be a good thing or a bad."

"It's all in the context you choose to take it," Dove said, fighting back a small smile. Wes narrowed his eyes and she smiled. "I studied philosophy at university."

Wes leaned back in his chair and put his hands over his eyes. "Oh, lord, not one of those. No *wonder*." Dove blinked back a sincere smile as she realised that he was joking. A moment later and he peered at her through his fingers and she couldn't help herself. She laughed. He grinned in return. "Well, I'm going to take it as a negative context, as that's what it was like most of the time. Imagine going to the market for some supper and being nearly assaulted by the young female employees. Or there was the time when I was nearly trapped in the hotel for three days because of the people waiting to ambush me outside. Not to mention airports."

Dove raised her eyebrows sympathetically. "Sounds terrible. I may only be a glorified barista, but at least I can get some quiet time if I so choose. I have part-time staff to help, after all."

"It's not all terrible," Wes said. "I mean the getting ambushed is, but I get paid well enough to afford people who will be discreet to get me from place to place. And my flat is quite nice."

"So you're happy to be rich but not famous," Dove nodded. "Are not the two things inherently connected?"

"You're definitely a philosopher. This is getting way to deep for a cheap Thai dinner," Wes said. Dove widened her eyes in apology. She immediately felt bad and knew that Wes was right. He was just taking her out to apologise for spilling her pastries and here she was getting into a philosophical conversation as though he were nothing more than a professor from university. That was probably the last thing he wanted, his co-worker analysing his life.

"I'm so sorry," Dove said, looking at her plate. "I didn't mean to—"

"That's not what I meant," Wes interjected firmly. "I meant that it's the sort of conversation to have over a glass of port and some lamb. Tomorrow?"

Dove looked at him in confusion. "What?" she asked. Was he asking her out again? Not as a date, certainly, but as a co-worker.

"I know this place you might like," Wes said. "It's

quiet and the people are discreet. The food is exquisite, too. What do you say?"

"Why are you doing this?" Dove asked. Wes nearly flinched at the quiet ice in her tone. "Do you pity me for today? Or am I some sort of novelty that you need to understand?"

"Yes, actually," Wes growled. He leaned his arm on the table and captured Dove's gaze with his own. "I have never seen anyone quite like you. You aren't afraid of people, yet you seem shy. You're intelligent and yet you hide behind the facade of being nothing more than a 'glorified barista'. And then there's your eyes."

"What is it with everyone and my eyes?" Dove asked. "They're blue, yes. There's nothing extraordinary about that. But it seems to be all that people are interested in. That's why Charlie hired me, he said. My eyes."

"The reason that everyone is so interested in your eyes is because they tell such a poignant story. Sad eyes aren't acted, Dove, they're created. There's a reason for it, and there's something about you that makes people want to figure out that reason. Me included," Wes said, his voice low. He maintained eye contact with Dove, and though she fidgeted, she couldn't bring herself to look away. "You're intriguing. Is it so bad that I want to have a conversation with you over dinner?"

Dove finally looked away, licking her lips nervously. Compliments weren't easy for her, probably because she had such a hard time believing them. "Just a conversation," she confirmed, stating the implied question.

"Just a conversation. We're going to be working together for a while. I'd like to know more about you. I've generally found it makes our jobs easier if we can understand the person across from us," Wes said. He sighed. "Look, Dove, I know that there's supposed to be this great romance between our characters, but all *I* want is understanding. If friendship develops from that, then fine, but I would settle for respect and understanding."

Dove studied Wes and decided she believed him. She had been so terrified of him earlier, when memories of her pain were fresh in her mind. Now, though, she believed that he might be one of the last people to hurt her. At least, not intentionally. So she nodded, "Okay. Understanding."

Wes smiled—a more true smile than the charming one he had been wearing for most of the day—and Dove let out a breath, relaxing and allowing herself to enjoy Thai food with the man.

7

———

"I still don't understand what you're doing here," Meg said, handing a drink over to a preteen who took it with a smile. Dove finished cleaning a stirring spoon and shrugged.

"I have the weekend, so I thought I'd come in and help. Keep from sitting still," Dove replied. She ignored Meg's incredulous look and set about arranging the pastry case. Rearranging, really.

"That's the most ridiculous story I've ever heard," Meg said. "You should be at home sleeping in instead of here."

"I thought you might want the help," Dove murmured. She ignored the quiet hurt that Meg's words dealt. She had hoped that Meg would want her around, but if not, then she would go home and memorise the script. But she just didn't want to be alone. Meg wrapped her arms around Dove and gave a tight squeeze.

"I'm *always* happy to have help," Meg said. "And even happier that you want to come in. I don't know how you managed this place on your own for so long."

"Only six months. And I wasn't alone. Rose comes in on Monday, Wednesdays, and Fridays to help," Dove pointed out. Meg just shook her head and went to deal with a customer while Dove made the drink. Once the man was gone, Meg slumped against the counter.

"Well, six months or not, you're completely insane. And you worked way too hard. I think I'm going to have to get someone else in to help, even with Rose. You know, to close up so I can get home for Timmy in the evenings." Meg lifted one shoulder in a shrug and Dove immediately felt badly for taking Meg's time away from her son.

"Of course," Dove said. "We'll put out an advert immediately. I'll write up a sign and we can put it in the window. Is his father giving you trouble?"

"He just doesn't like Timmy having to hang around the cafe instead of being at home. He says that he'd rather Timmy was with him than hanging around here," Meg sighed. "I need this job, but I can't lose my son to that man."

"Well, we'll get someone in and in a week or so, you can leave earlier," Dove said. "You're the manager, now, Meg. You don't really need my permission to do anything. Unless you want to, you know, start serving fried courgette. Then we might have a problem."

Meg laughed—exactly the reaction Dove wanted— and the two went back to work as the morning rush started picking up. "So, tell me again, why did you cancel your dinner with Weston Blackwood last night?" Meg asked, steaming some milk. The older woman waiting for her drink raised her eyebrows and Dove blushed.

"Perhaps we could just call him Wes," she murmured to Meg. "We don't need the world descending on the cafe."

"Good point," Meg said, handing over the mocha with a smile. The woman lingered for a moment, as if she wanted to hear more, but Meg resolutely waited until she walked away before turning to Dove with a raised eyebrow. "Okay, so, cancelling dinner with Wes?"

"It was all just a bit much," Dove said. "I got poked and prodded, had multiple rounds of makeup put on and taken off, had lights flashed in my eyes, went through I don't know how many different outfits. On top of the reading on Thursday, I just needed an evening to myself. I don't think he minded, though."

"That's the worst excuse for cancelling a date that I've ever heard," Meg said firmly, practically glowering. "You are in an entirely different world, now. You have to embrace these things as they come. Or you're going to end up cynical and bitter like me."

"You're the least cynical person I know," Dove pointed out. Meg shook her head.

"I can be perfectly cynical. For example, that man who fathered my son is a right proper—"

"I don't think that counts," Dove cut in, glancing

pointedly at the two people descending on the register to order. Meg took the orders and turned back to Dove, who was already preparing the croissants.

"You never answered my question," Meg said. "Why did you cancel the date?"

"I'm not certain it was a date," Dove said. Meg, for all that she was five years older than Dove, knew her better than Dove knew herself sometimes. Or, better than Dove would have liked to admit. All it took for Dove to backpedal was Meg raising her eyebrows. "It was because it was a date. On top of everything else, that's the last thing I wanted."

"Are you sure about that? You said yourself that you two shared a relaxing and pleasant conversation over Thai food. Would going on a date with him really have been that bad?" Meg asked.

Dove folded her arms and hunched her shoulders, indecisive. She looked desperately at Meg and finally shook her head, her chestnut hair falling into her face. "Honestly, I don't know. I haven't dated for... a really long time."

Meg softened her gaze and reached out to squeeze Dove's shoulder comfortingly. "I know. Oh, Dove, I know. Not all men are like him, you know. Like those two bastards—don't you give me that look, you know it's true and there is no one listening. Come on, Dove, you have to put yourself out there. Maybe Wes will be just the sort you need. Unless you think he's too old or he's really arrogant or something."

"It's not that. Age doesn't matter to me," Dove said.

"It's more about a meeting of minds. And he's not arrogant, despite being known to just about every woman. It's... well, everything. My issues combined with the fact that he's a professional actor."

"What does that have to do with anything?"

Dove gave up on even pretending to work, instead letting Meg handle the customers. Instead, she leaned against the counter and tried not to shout her problems out to the customers wanting their drinks and food. It was getting on past the morning rush, but there were still enough people to make talking a sensitive topic. Maybe she just didn't want to talk about it at all. Dove knew her issues perfectly well and wanted to avoid them as best she could. "What if nothing he says is genuine? What if he only wants to get close to me because I'm costarring? How can I trust—"

"Stop right there," Meg said, planting her hands on her hips. The man paying for his drink coughed politely in the back of his throat, but Meg ignored him. Dove pushed herself away from the counter and started on the drink. It was one thing that she knew how to do, bury her problems in work. Focusing on herself for more than a few moments was something she couldn't manage. Meg caught on and finished serving the man, but as soon as he walked away, she rounded on Dove again.

"Don't you dare pull the trust card, Dove Graves," Meg said in an undertone. "I thought we'd been over this. Not all men are like those fools. This Wes seems genuinely nice and you said you had a good time at dinner. You can't hide in your fears forever."

Dove said nothing. There was nothing to say, because she both knew that Meg was right and feared that she would be proven wrong. It was safer to keep her walls up and hide behind her work. Why get involved with a coworker? It was a well-known fact that such things only led to trouble. Especially with actors. "You're blowing this way out of proportion," Dove said at last. "We don't even know what his intentions were in regards to taking me out."

"If he didn't want to take you on a date, then I'm up for parliament," Meg grumbled. Dove shook her head wryly.

"I didn't realise you were interested in politics," she murmured. Meg caught her eye and started laughing, nearly scaring the young boy and his mother in for their morning treat.

"Alright, you win. We'll talk about something else," Meg said. "How about you go get that help wanted sign made up?"

"Whatever you say, boss," Dove said, letting her own smile shine. It was small and didn't quite meet her eyes, but it was as genuine as any she ever gave. She slipped off to the back room and the tiny office at the back of the kitchen, getting to work on seeking a new employee to help Meg. Dove threw herself into the task, simple as it was, as a release from her worries. It was done too quickly, but there was the kitchen to tidy up and things to organise. She moved from one task to the next, doing each with a vigour that she never normally held for that cafe. It didn't matter how meaningless the job, as long as it kept her occupied.

After she had emptied the half-full rubbish bin out back, Dove sat at the chair in the office and conceded the fact that she was running away. Everything Meg had said was true. She was afraid that Wes was interested in her because of her history with men. She was also afraid that she would never 'get out there', as Meg had claimed. Perhaps Wes was the way to do that. It didn't have to mean anything serious, just two people having a good time. As friends, and if something more developed, then something more developed. First, though, Dove had to stop shying away from his touch, both physical and metaphorical.

"Dove," Meg called out, startling Dove from her thoughts. She stood and walked out to the main area, planning to help with a sudden rush of people. Instead, a man stood off to one side, glowering, with Meg's son at his side. Meg looked at Dove helplessly before turning to Timmy's father.

"What are you doing here, Jim?" Meg stepped out from behind the counter, letting Dove take over serving the single person in the queue. Jim, a hulking man with more weight around his middle than muscle and a thinning hairline, frowned deeper. Timmy lunged for his mother and wrapped his arms around her leg.

"Hi, Mummy!" he said, looking up at her with a smile. Dove let herself smile, too, for a moment, at the simple joy the boy had. The customer took her drink and left, leaving the four of them alone. Dove stepped around the counter herself and waved to Timmy while ignoring his father. This man was another one of the sort that set her spine to tingling.

"We need to talk," Jim spat. Meg glared and pushed Timmy in Dove's direction.

"Timmy, can you stay with Dove for a minute? Your daddy and I are going to go have a quiet word," Meg said. Timmy eagerly took Dove's hand, simultaneously shooting his parents a worried look over his shoulder. Meg led Jim through the cafe and out the back door, into an alleyway where no one would overhear. Dove moved over to the pastry case.

"Would you like a strudel, Timmy? I have apple and cherry." Dove pointed to the treats, but the boy just shrugged.

"Mummy and Daddy are fighting again," he said matter-of-factly. "I don't like it when they fight."

"Sometimes people just don't get along." Dove soothed as best she could, knowing full well her words wouldn't help at all. She just put a comforting hand on Timmy's shoulder and let the boy lean into her leg. They stood like that until the door to the cafe opened. Dove turned to greet the customer and faltered. Wes was shrugging off his jacket, calm and stunningly handsome with his hair blown from the wind outside. He took one look at Dove and grinned.

"I finally found your cafe," Wes said, moving in closer. Timmy poked his head out from around Dove's legs and stared up at the newcomer. It was Wes' turn to falter; he stared at Timmy with the same unabashed shock that Timmy showed him. Wes blinked and flicked his eyes to Dove, asking a silent question.

Dove blushed slightly at the implication, though her voice betrayed none of her embarrassment. Maybe acting was paying off. "Timmy, this is Wes, someone I work with. Wes, this is Timmy. His mother is the person who is running the cafe in my absence. She stepped out for a moment."

"Ah," Wes said, relaxing his shoulders slightly. "A pleasure to meet you, Timmy. Were you about to get a pastry?"

"Dove always gives me a treat when I come in," Timmy declared. Wes smiled knowingly and the boy continued. "I'm going to have a studel."

"Strudel," Dove corrected absently. She walked around the counter and pulled out her tongs. "Apple or cherry?"

Timmy looked between the two options, frowning with fierce concentration. He looked up at Wes for assistance and the actor crouched next to the boy. "They both look good, don't they?" Wes asked. Timmy nodded. "Well, I don't know about you, but I like apple. Especially with a cup of cocoa."

The young boy looked up at Dove, hopeful. She responded with an indulgent smile. "Just as long as you tell your mother the cocoa was *his* idea, not mine," Dove said. She pulled out the two pastries and started on the drinks, making the hot chocolate with a touch of cinnamon. Timmy took his treats to a table and started devouring the strudel. Wes leaned against the counter and sipped thoughtfully at his drink.

"What's his story?" he nodded at the boy and turned to Dove. She frowned and swiped at the machines with a damp cloth.

"I don't really think it's any of your business," she murmured so Timmy wouldn't overhear. Wes held up his hands as a sign that he would back off. "I'm sorry," Dove apologised. "It's just that his parents are having difficulties. It's not really my place to tell anything."

"I understand. I just think that he really seems to admire you. Not to mention your pastries—" Wes was broken off by the sound of the back door slamming. Dove winced and shrank into herself, knowing full well what was coming. Jim strode through the kitchen and the main part of the cafe, muttering angrily under his breath. He spotted Dove and curled his lip.

"If it weren't for me, that bitch would be on the streets," he snarled, jabbing a finger in Dove's direction. She took a half-step backwards. Wes straightened and looked at Jim with an expression that could curdle milk.

"Sir," he said, making it quite clear that he didn't believe Jim deserved that moniker, "I think it would be best if you left."

"Don't worry," Jim hissed. "I'm leaving." He glowered for a moment longer then stalked out of the cafe, ignoring the quiet call his son sent after him. The cafe door swung shut and Dove let out a breath. She hated dealing with Jim, but there was little Meg could do to keep him away from Timmy. She needed the extra income that Jim's child-support provided. Even managing the cafe would barely cover the bills.

Meg shuffled back into the cafe, her face directed at the floor. At Timmy's querulous cry after his father, she broke out of her own misery and ran to her son, kneeling and wrapping him in her arms. "It's okay, sweet. Mummy's here," Meg soothed. Timmy hugged his mother and she nearly broke down.

Dove stepped over and put her hand on Meg's shoulder. "Timmy, do you think that you could show Wes the board games over in the corner by the fireplace?" Timmy cheered up immediately and grabbed Wes' hand, pulling him over to the chairs in the back corner. Meg sat in a chair and Dove went to turn the sign on the cafe door to closed. This was obviously a conversation that wouldn't withstand customers interrupting.

"He's getting married," Meg said, wiping her eyes with the heel of her palm. Meg laughed drily. "I'm not surprised about that. There was always one woman or another, after all. Now, he's gone and got the wrong girl pregnant and her father is making him marry."

"Do you think it will calm him down?" Dove asked softly. Meg shook her head and laughed again, the sound grating and defeated.

"Jim? Not a chance. No, the problem is that his newfound bride doesn't want anything to do with his former family. Jim doesn't want Timmy around anymore. And apparently, his new father-in-law has access to considerable legal services. Because we were never married, the child-support that Jim is paying is not legally binding. That's going away." Meg started crying in earnest.

"Hey, it's going to be alright," Dove said, grabbing Meg's hand and squeezing it. The other woman smiled and more tears slipped from her eyes. "You just got a great new job with a pay raise from your old job. You don't need his money."

"Even with the new salary, I'll barely be able to pay for Timmy's needs and groceries and such. I... I won't be able to afford the flat anymore," Meg breathed, desperation putting an edge into her voice. Dove paled. She hadn't realised things were quite so bad. Maybe with her own salary from the film, she could do something more. Better pay, maybe. The only problem was, she hadn't actually got paid yet. It would come much, much later. She couldn't leave Meg out in the cold, though.

"How long will you have?" Dove asked.

"The end of the month is in two days. I won't be able to make next month's rent. So maybe a week, if the landlord is feeling generous?" Meg covered her eyes with her hands and let her shoulders shake. "How could he be so heartless?"

"Men are like that," Dove said with more bite than she had intended.

Meg jerked her head upwards and shook her head, sniffling. "No," she said. "Not all men. Just the one's we've known."

"If you were any more of a romantic, you'd be in a film yourself." Dove tried to lighten the mood, but all she managed to do was get Meg to start laughing while crying. The tears came faster. "Look, Meg, I know that things are difficult for you. Why don't you come live with me? I have a spare bedroom. It's not much, but I'll be busy working on the film and it would be great to have you and Timmy around."

Meg gaped at Dove. "You can't be serious."

"Why not?" Dove asked. Meg started to open her mouth and interject a dozen excuses, but Dove held up her hand. "I have the space and you have the need. You are one of the few people I would even *consider* having come stay with me. Not to mention that I might need to spend the night at the warehouse sometimes. It would be a waste to let the space go unused."

Meg smiled through her tears, though this time they were from gratitude. "You are the best person I know. Thank you."

Dove merely nodded in acknowledgement, the compliment making her uncomfortable. She stood and wandered over to the back of the cafe where Timmy was attempting to play Scrabble with Wes. The boy was complaining that Wes wasn't using real words. When Dove looked at the board, she had to agree. "Thyrol?" she asked. "What in the world is that?"

"I have no idea," Wes said. Timmy gaped openly at the actor. He huffed and grumbled that Wes didn't understand the game. He stalked over to his mother to complain, leaving Dove and Wes to clean up the game. "I, well, I overheard," Wes said softly. Dove raised her eyebrows. "It's difficult not to with no one else in here."

"One of the faults of this place," Dove agreed, lowering her own voice. "Please don't say anything. Meg has enough problems."

"I won't. I do have one question, though," Wes said. Dove nodded as a go-ahead. "Can you really be that good of a person?"

"What?" Dove asked. She shoved the Scrabble box back onto the shelf and perched on the arm of one of the chairs. "You mean letting Meg stay at my flat? She's my friend. Isn't that what friends do?"

"My friends pushed me into taking this job without any consideration of what I wanted," Wes growled lowly. Dove blinked, and he shook his head. "Never mind. It's just that you don't often find people willing to give so selflessly. It's a nice change from some of the people I deal with."

"Thank you, I guess," Dove murmured. "Though I don't think that people are nearly as bad as you make them out to be. Not *all* of them, that is."

"You intrigue me, Dove," Wes replied. "One minute you're carrying the weight of the world on your shoulders and trying not to show your disappointment with lost dreams. The next, you're defending the human race against chronic cynics like me."

"I'm not that complicated," Dove shrugged. She stood to return to work and Wes caught her hand, keeping her still. Dove tensed, ready to fight and pull away. But his grip never tightened beyond a comfortable touch and his skin against hers felt good. Really good.

She swallowed quietly, wondering why that felt stranger than her panic.

"Have dinner with me," Wes said, staring straight into Dove's eyes, keeping her locked in place. He blinked slowly, and though there was no smile, the effect was just as breathtaking. "Not as colleagues or even pleasant acquaintances. A date. A real date."

"Wes..." Dove started, looking away. Wes brushed his thumb over her hand and she looked at him again, somehow unable to keep away for long. "I don't know if—"

"You had a valid excuse last night. It was a long day for everyone. Don't give me another excuse. Or is it that you don't want to go on a date with me?" Wes asked, his eyes darkening, though not with anger. Dove blinked and licked her suddenly dry lips.

"It's not that," she breathed.

"Good," Wes growled, standing and looking down into Dove's eyes. "Then I'll stop by your flat at seven. See you then."

Without so much as a by-your-leave, he dropped Dove's hand and walked out of the cafe, giving a wave to Timmy and a nod to Meg. Dove remained where she was, not entirely certain of what had just happened. She was under the general impression that it was good, though, so there was that.

8

Curious as he was about this turn of events with Dove, Wes was prompt. He had wheedled her address out of Marc and even bought a flower. A purple iris, which the florist said meant wisdom and compliments, or something equally ridiculous. He only knew that it seemed to suit Dove. He had dressed for the part in black slacks and a grey shirt, even taking the time to shower and shave. All of this meant that as soon as he put his foot on the stair to walk up to the second floor, he couldn't fathom what was going on in his mind.

Wash had specifically asked Wes to seduce Dove. To date Dove. To make her feel more comfortable, especially about doing a romance. Reluctantly, Wes had agreed. Dove was more than ten years younger than him and the general idea of such a disparity had been the issue from the beginning. Now he was going out of his way to buy a flower and think about his appearance—more than usual, that is—because he found her intriguing. She was pretty and intelligent and had the most fascinating eyes he had ever seen. But that didn't mean he should go and *actually* get emotionally involved with Dove. He was just supposed to make her time on set easier. Make her less uncomfortable when they basically had sex—even with discreet coverings for the intimate places of the body—for the cameras to see. He was not meant to find himself actually interested in her.

Wes had to remind himself that he hadn't wanted to do this in the first place. And, as he was walking up the stairs, he kept running the thought through his head: *fourteen years.* The age difference between them eventually overrode any potential interest he might have had. By the time he reached out to knock on her door, Wes had to put on his acting mask to seem as interested as he had a moment ago.

"There's something wrong with you," Wes muttered to himself. He knew exactly from where all of this was coming, even if he was only focusing on part of it. The dark times, out of which came a bitter man owing a favour to Charles Wash. He never wanted to go through that sort of ruinous emotional attachment again. Certainly not with a child like Dove.

Then, the door opened.

The first things he noticed were her legs. They were bare up to the middle of her thigh and were perfectly sculpted, smooth and pale. The hem of her bluish-grey dress brushed her legs loosely, creating tantalising shadows. The dress was nothing more than a shirt-dress, cinched at the waist with a brown leather belt, but it showed off every curve that Dove Graves had while simultaneously leaving enough to Wes' imagination to make him swallow with need. The dress had a generally modest neckline, leaving Wes to wonder and imagine stunning things. Her hair had been left down, the chestnut strands framing her face and brushing her shoulders. She wore no makeup, but she didn't need it. The blues in her dress brought out her eyes and her lips were naturally lush.

Pretty? Wes thought with a shudder down his spine. No, she was beautiful. And as for being a child, even that was soundly disregarded. With a look like that, a dangerously sultry smile that was both warming and sad, legs up to the sky and eyes that could see into a man's soul, there was no way Wes could think of her as a child ever again. Fourteen years? He could live with that.

"Hi," Dove said, her smile brightening ever-so-slightly as she took Wes in. He tried to stop staring. Dove began to fidget, tugging the hem of her dress down. "Um, is this alright? I didn't know where you had planned to go, but I didn't want to be too dressed up. I can change, if—"

"It's fine," Wes assured her. He pulled his eyes over her pointedly, making certain that she knew his thoughts. He was pleased when a blush spread into Dove's cheeks. He had made absolutely sure she knew that this was a real date, and he wasn't going to let her forget it. Not even if Wash had been the one to force Wes to do this.

In a flash, the pleasure Wes had felt surging through him at the sight of Dove was tarnished. It was still there —he couldn't deny that, now—but he felt dirty. It was as if he was sullying Dove. She didn't deserve that. He couldn't walk away. Not only because Wash had demanded it of him, but because Wes knew that something wonderful would be lost forever if he did.

"So, you're not going to tell me where we're going, then," Dove said, filling in for Wes' silence. He smirked and shook his head.

"No, but you might want a jacket," he replied. "As much as I'd hate to have that dress covered, it is actually cold outside."

Dove reached back and pulled a dark peacoat off the hook by the door. She slung a small bag across her body and stepped into the hall, closing the door behind her. Wes chuckled and stepped aside to let her pass, putting his hand on the small of her back to guide her.

"You are certainly prepared," he said. Dove nodded, brushing a strand of hair from her face.

"I believe in being prepared for every eventuality," she said. "Though becoming an actress and walking away wasn't at the top of my mental list of eventualities."

"It usually isn't," Wes agreed. He handed her the flower and was immediately pleased when Dove brought it to her nose and inhaled its delicate scent, an expression of true joy on her face.

"It's beautiful, thank you." Dove took another deep breath, the petals of the flower tickling her nose. Instead of putting the flower back in her flat, Dove tucked it into the crook of her arm. Wes didn't know why this made him smile, but it did. A real smile, too, not one of his various acting smiles.

He led her into a silver town car waiting by the curb and waited until the door was closed before answering her confused expression. "It turns out that taking a taxi or an Uber when you are a famous movie star is a really good way to get people to figure out where you are. This company is on retainer with Wash and is very good with being discreet."

"It's like another world," Dove said. "Having such resources at your disposal."

"Money doesn't buy happiness," Wes said the old adage with the eloquence of someone who had said such things many times before. Dove shook her head.

"No," she agreed. "It doesn't. But it does buy opportunity."

Wes was silent for a moment, rolling her words over in his head. Then, he nodded and settled deeper into the seat. "I keep forgetting that you're far wiser than someone your age has a right to be."

"Someone my age? You do realise that I've been to university and was running my own business before this career change?" Dove said. Wes feared he had offended her for a moment, but he saw the amusement in her smile and let out a breath.

"When I was your age, all I cared about was dressing well, dating well, eating well and living well. I had just recently got a larger role, and I had every possible resource I could want. Women were easy to find and people were in awe of me. I don't know if a wise word ever came out of my mouth until I was in my thirties." Wes put on a friendly wince at his terrible behaviour, but he wasn't exaggerating. Those years had been essential to building his career, but they had been empty of everything except acting experience. And, the foolish decisions he had made led him into the dark times, something he wished he could forget. Desperately.

"Wisdom doesn't come with age," Dove countered. "It comes with experience. Maybe I've just had more experience than you did."

"Are you saying that I'm not doing a good job at living my life?" Wes asked wryly. He watched the skin on Dove's cheeks flush with embarrassment and was pleased that he could bring out such a reaction.

"No, of course not," she defended, aghast. "I just meant.. well, we've had different styles of living and... erm. I just.."

"Dove, it's alright," Wes said, reaching out to brush a strand of her hair back. She looked at him desperately and he nodded, confirming his words. "I was just teasing you."

She shot him a reproachful look, and he just

chuckled. Dove was silent for a moment, making Wes wonder if he'd gone too far. Teasing her had seemed so natural and he thought that she could handle it, would even laugh, but perhaps those sad eyes were holding something more than they seemed. "One of these days," Dove said, quiet mischief in her voice, "I'm going to get you back for that."

Wes let his shoulders slump in relief. "What, no witty comeback?" he teased again, this time enjoying it fully.

Dove huffed, "I read philosophy, not theatre. It takes me a minute sometimes."

"I'll allow that. Okay, Dove," We sat up at the slowing of the car. "We're here."

"Where is here?" Dove asked. Wes said nothing, now certain that his plan for the evening would go over well. She was the sort to do and enjoy unusual things. After all, she had picked herself up from her cafe to a lifestyle completely different from her own because someone had asked her. She was careful, perhaps, in her recklessness, but the edge was there. That didn't change the fact that Wes enjoyed the look of confusion on Dove's face when she climbed from the car and looked at the building.

"Green Vale Retirement Centre?" Dove sounded skeptical. Wes nodded and took her arm, following an older man with a walker into the building.

"It's bingo night," Wes said by way of explanation. Dove raised her eyebrows and looked at the brick building. "It's one of the few places that I can come without being recognised. Besides, you're going to have quite the competition. These people take their bingo very seriously."

Dove said nothing, only tightened her grip ever-so-slightly on Wes' arm. He felt a surge of pleasure at the motion and led his date through the building to the dining hall, where the game was to be held.

The building itself was nothing special. It wasn't high end or rundown, it was just a nice centre with decent carpets, worn-but-quality furniture, paintings of seascapes on the walls and the ever-present smell of detergent. The dining hall had round tables with eight chairs around each table. There were quite a few people gathered for bingo night, talking with one another and getting their boards. There were even a few families visiting, the younger people standing out.

Wes led Dove to a table in a relatively secluded corner, holding out the chair for her. She sat and was almost immediately joined by three seniors: two men and one woman. Wes slipped into the chair next to Dove. She was nervously organising her selection of chips into colour categories, arranging them around her board.

"You look as though you have a strategy all planned out," the man sitting closest to Dove said. He was wearing an old Pringle fisherman's sweater and leaned one hand on a cane. "Don't you worry, love, I've been playing this game for years. If you need any help, just ask Old William."

Dove smiled gently. "I'll be sure to do that. I've been told that this game can get rather competitive."

"Oh yes." William nodded his head firmly and pointed his cane in the general direction of the table holding the microphone and cage with the numbers. "See those women up over there? The ones all dressed in green? They're very determined. Think that sitting closer to the announcer gives them a better chance."

"Goodness," Dove replied, peering over Wes' shoulder to catch a glimpse of the women. Wes wanted to reach out and brush the hair that swung forwards, just to feel it. He had brought Dove here to be unique and because it was actually one of the few places he could go without a huge fuss being made, but now he was beginning to regret the fact that he hadn't taken her dancing. Then, he could be quite a lot closer to her than the current seating arrangement allowed. "There must be quite the prize."

"There is," the woman at the table confirmed with a firm nod. She had a head full of bouncy curls in a bright, fire-engine red and looked eager for the game to begin. "It's a certificate for that nice restaurant, The Wooden Rose. It's the second one to open, since the first one, all the way in New York City, was so well received. You can't get in without a reservation."

Dove raised her eyebrows and turned her face to her card, obviously fighting back a smile. Wes took the opportunity to slide his chair closer to Dove so he could whisper in her ear. "If you'd rather go somewhere else," he murmured, "then we can. I thought that you might enjoy this, though."

"This is great, really," Dove replied. "You're the only person I've ever met who would come up with an idea like this. It's unique. And now I'm determined to see if I can't win that certificate."

Wes chuckled. "I never would have thought you the competitive type."

"I can be competitive when the need arises." Dove shrugged. "I don't know why you find that surprising, considering I ran my own business."

Wes bit back the retort that she had inherited her business and, from what Wash had told him, didn't really care all that much about the cafe. Instead, he just leaned his shoulder against hers and said nothing, preferring to watch as she talked politely with William and the woman, asking about their bingo experiences. She was just as capable here as she was in the cafe and during the reading. Still, though, her smile never quite reached her eyes.

Dove Graves was a mystery to Wes. He had met few women—few people in general—with as many facets as she had. She had given up her life to act for Wash, stepping into the complete unknown to pursue something that might get her away from a place that had never been her dream. She had seemed unfazed by the fame of Wes and the people around her. She had helped her friend and her friend's son without a second thought. Tonight, she was okay with his casual touch against her shoulder or hair. And yet, she had fled at Wes' touch once before, taking the necessary measures to distance herself. He didn't believe her story about food poisoning for one minute.

He did believe that the emotion of the scene might have been a bit too much for her. She hadn't done this before and showing that depth to people she had never met must be difficult. In that regard, Wes understood completely why Wash wanted him to seduce her. He just wished that he didn't feel like he was double crossing her.

Because Wes wanted this.

The start of the game pulled him from his thoughts and he joined in, not really caring whether he won or not. It was merely enough to watch Dove listen for the number and letter and carefully put her chip down on the appropriate square. William congratulated her over every placed chip and whistled when she missed out on bingo by one. Then, Dove flicked her eyes over to Wes' card and nudged him in the side.

"If you don't call out 'bingo' now, then one of those ladies up there is going to win that certificate," Dove said. Sure enough, Wes had a complete row. He started to open his mouth when, just as Dove predicted, one of the ladies crowed her victory and shouted out "Bingo!" to the whole room.

There were some people grumbling their disappointment, but Wes just laughed. Dove smiled, too. "I'll let her have it," Wes said. "I don't need a certificate to go to The Wooden Rose. If you're interested, we can go tonight."

"You don't need to do that," Dove murmured. "I'm not one of those people that expects a five-star restaurant on a first date."

Wes pulled back, shaking his head. He knew that. It was so essentially Dove. That didn't mean he didn't want to give it to her. "I didn't think you were. Listen, Dove, I'm going to say this now so it doesn't cause problems in the future. I'm rich. Really rich. This film isn't even going to make it as one of the larger grossing films I've done and I'm still getting paid one and a half million pounds. That's nothing to me. I don't think you care about the money, but I just wanted you to know that I'm taking you out to wherever because I want to do so, not because I'm showing off."

If he expected his speech to shock Dove, Wes was mistaken. All she did was furrow her brows and blush slightly, saying, "And I thought *I* was getting paid well for the film."

Wes laughed and ignored the glares from the seniors around him listening fervently to the bingo caller. "You have a ways to go, love," Wes shook his head. He got a furious shush from the woman across the table and Wes stood, deciding it would be easier to talk to Dove if they weren't surrounded by people intent on their game. She didn't complain, merely whispered farewell to their table mates and left as she had come in, her arm entwined in his.

Wes enjoyed the heat of her body, feeling her touch as an acute sensation. It felt odd for a moment until he realised that he was actually enjoying her touch as though he were a randy teenager again. She excited feelings in him that he hadn't felt in a long time. The way she looked at him openly, smiling and unafraid, undaunted by him was electrifying. And when she licked lips that had dried in the slight wind, Wes wanted to take them as his own.

They walked for a block before Wes couldn't resist any longer. He stopped and pulled Dove around to face him. For a moment, she tensed up, but when he just looked into her eyes, running his hands up and down her arms, she relaxed again. The blue depths were wide and searching and, yes, sad. But a moment later, as he continued to stare at her, that vanished. Dove's pupils dilated—a purely physical show of desire—and Wes grinned his victory.

Wes leaned in and cupped Dove's face, pulling her lips to his and possessing her. Gently, he kissed her, the touch more of a brush than a true display of passion. He tested her. Tasted her. She tasted like honey and immediately, Wes was addicted. When Dove sighed and relaxed further into his arms, Wes knew that was the end of it.

Wash and his plans be damned. Wes was getting close to Dove for his own sake.

The kiss left Dove feeling breathless. Not in a bad, fearful way, either. No, she was about as far as she could get from the panic attack that hat hit her only a couple of days before. Her heart felt as though it had stopped, and yet she couldn't help but hear it pounding in her ears. Wes' lips against hers was dramatic, to say the least. There was heat and pressure building up from who-knows-where and expressing itself in the way that Dove clutched the fabric of his shirt in desperation or the way she moaned in the back of her throat when his tongue entered her mouth, pressing for dominance.

Wes pulled back after she had let the sound slip and grinned at her with half-lidded eyes, making it perfectly clear what he wanted to do. If Dove had doubted his intentions, wondering if he were only doing this because he was working with her for the next while, then that theory had flown out the window. She still felt a little shaky, standing on wobbling legs.

"Weston Blackwood?" a voice asked and immediately, the sexual tension that hung between Dove and Wes vanished, turning into something far icier. Wes stiffened, though he kept a hand on Dove's shoulder, and turned. Dove peered over his shoulder to find a girl—she must have been a teenager—holding a phone and staring wide-eyed at Wes. She was also taking pictures.

Wes cursed and rounded on the teenager with a snarl. "Who are you?" he demanded, stalking up to her. The girl's eyes grew impossibly wider, and she stumbled backwards, shrinking into herself. "Why are you here? Why were you taking pictures?" Wes growled furiously. The girl started shaking, probably from fear of coming face to face with such an attractive, famous man, especially one that looked as though he were about to bite her head off.

"Wes," Dove murmured, barely loud enough for him to hear. His attention shifted, though, and he looked at Dove with apologetic frustration. He didn't realise he was scaring the girl. Not unintelligent, though, the teenager lifted her phone and snapped a few more pictures before turning and running off like a cheetah. Dove doubted that even Wes, for all his well-toned muscles and marathon training, could have caught up with her.

Wes cursed again and clenched his fists at his side. He watched the girl go with a tick in his jaw and didn't even relax when Dove came up to him and touched his shoulder gently. "I'm sorry," he snarled, obviously not apologising for his behaviour, but for the girl. "I tried to go to a place where no one would know me and I wouldn't be recognised or photographed or anything. Now our picture is going to be plastered all over the internet."

"You can't blame yourself for that," Dove murmured, though she felt her heart beating faster at the thought of her picture on the internet. After a moment, the beat calmed. What did she have to fear from that? Social media was a constant, and while Dove was not the sort to take selfies and make videos, even she had friends put pictures of her online. Mostly from her university days, but still. It wasn't a big deal.

Only, Wes seemed to think it was.

"I can blame myself, though. I should have just ordered take away and we could have played board games at my flat. Or the warehouse. And now, not only are you in the spotlight, but Wash is going to kill me, too. He wanted publicity low until filming was well under way. He wanted to keep you a secret," Wes hissed. He took a deep breath and let it out through his nose, obviously trying to calm down.

Dove said nothing for a moment, not entirely sure she could be trusted not to make things worse. This was plainly a sore point with Wes. She wasn't terribly thrilled with the idea of being caught up in the fame, either. But her feelings mattered little. "It's done, Wes. There's nothing you can do and you can't honestly blame yourself for a chance run-in with a fan. I'll be alright. Wash is the one who is going to need therapy."

Wes shot Dove an incredulous look and frowned. "He's going to be pissed."

"I would think that after having directed however-many movies he's directed and dealt with famous actors and the press, not to mention social media during that time that Wash would be used to it," Dove said. "You're the one who seems upset."

"I'd have taken her phone if I could," Wes murmured.

"And done what? She'd have called the police and you would have an even bigger issue," Dove pointed out. "Besides, surely you've dealt with this sort of thing before."

Wes ran his hand over his head, letting out a frustrated sound. "You have no idea," he said. "But I've been dealing with this for years. You haven't. I wanted to keep you out of this as much as I could. Keep you away from the parasites that are going to try and find out every piece of your history, figure out what it is that made Wash pick *you*, why I'm with *you*."

Dove paled slightly at the description of the press. Parasites certainly seemed to fit. She hadn't liked the thought of being caught up in the recognition that would come with being in a film, but she also knew that it was part of that world. After this was over, she wouldn't have to do it again and, eventually, she would be forgotten. The idea of the press digging into her past, though, uncovering all of her childhood memories and bringing back people that she had tried to forget, made her freeze. The beginnings of a panic attack roiled up through her and her breath hitched.

"Dove?" Wes asked, concern in his voice. "Are you alright?"

Dove focused her thoughts and pushed the panic down. There was nothing she could do to stop the digging, but her life was as far from public as she could make it. No social media, no blogs, nothing. Her friends might have pictures online, but that was something entirely different than what Wes was talking about. Suddenly, her earlier thoughts seemed far too cavalier. She couldn't worry about the rest of the world right now. Wes, though, was standing a mere foot away, looking as though he feared for her safety. Her mind turned to the kiss he had given her a few minutes before and she smiled.

"I'm fine," she murmured. "I'm just... I'm sorry this upset you. I understand if you want to just go home."

Wes stiffened, staring at Dove in shock. "You want to go home?"

Dove shook her head, licking her lips to evoke the taste of him again. "No," she breathed. "Not really. Not after... but you're probably thinking that this whole thing was a bad idea. Look at the mess I've got us into."

Wes surprised Dove, proving yet again that her fears were unfounded, persistent though they were. He stepped forwards and wrapped his arms around her, pulling her as close to him as she could get. She turned her face to press her cheek against his shoulder and inhaled quietly, memorising his scent. It was subtle and thoroughly masculine. "If I can't be blamed for what happened," Wes murmured in her ear, "then there is no way that this is your fault. I do not want to go home, Dove. Not without you."

Dove smiled, letting out a quiet and subdued laugh. "So what do we do now?"

"It's been a trying evening." Wes brushed his hand over her hair. "How about we order some food and go to the warehouse? I'd invite you home, but it might be a bit too soon for that." Dove nodded quiet agreement.

"Do you think there's a sandwich shop still open this late?" Dove asked while Wes dialled the number for the driver to come fetch them. He frowned and shrugged. "Well, there's always Tesco."

Wes smiled. "I'm sure we can find something better than Tesco."

Dove shrugged, mirroring his gesture. He wrapped his arm around her shoulder and rubbed her arm to keep her warm, though Dove would have been more than happy with just his touch. It seemed to send electricity through her system. She knew she should be wary, but she couldn't bring herself to be so.

Twenty minutes later and the glow still hadn't worn off. They found themselves alone in the warehouse, sitting in Wes' dressing room, which Dove explored with interest while Wes set out the food they had scrounged from a local Pret a Manger. She ran her fingers lightly over the speakers and the dock for his phone and wondered what sort of music he listened to.

He was older than she was, not to mention better connected to such things, and probably knew of some more interesting, obscure bands. Or maybe he listened to classical. Somehow, though, Dove pictured him as more of a classic, high-quality rock sort of person.

"You know, when you were first introduced to me as the person I would be acting with," Wes said, causing Dove to turn and look at him, suddenly feeling shy, "I had no idea that this would be the result."

"What? Us hiding out in the warehouse?" she asked lightly, sitting on the couch facing him. He smirked and shook his head, reaching out to brush his hand against her knee. Dove swallowed.

"Well, that, but also you just... being you." Dove furrowed her brows in confusion, though, admittedly, part of her mind was occupied with the patterns he was drawing on her skin. "I've acted with a lot of people, and you'd be surprised how many of them are interested in money and fame and nothing more. The older I've got, the worse the ones entering into the world seem to get. I dreaded the young woman I'd be paired with when I read the script, thinking she'd be some air-headed baby, desperate for a shot at fame and fortune, especially with me."

Dove laughed drily, blushing at the unspoken compliment and not quite sure how to deal with it. "You got me instead," she said with a half-shrug. Wes leaned in and brushed his lips against her forehead, making her breath hitch.

"Exactly," he murmured. "You're nothing like I

expected. I do have to ask you something, though." He pulled away and Dove instinctively did the same. She'd done something wrong. She knew it. This was too good to last. Either he'd be the issue or she would. Wes grabbed her hand before she could retreat to the complete opposite end of the couch and held her there, rubbing his thumb lightly over her skin, his eyes cast downwards. "Does it bother you that I'm nearly fifteen years older than you?"

Dove blinked, not expecting that. She'd thought that he had found her like the other people he had described. Desperate, air-headed. She pushed the thought away and looked at him, noticing the slight line between his eyebrows that betrayed his worry. "Does it bother you?" she asked quietly.

Wes lifted his head and shot her an accusing, but affectionate, look. "Now that's not fair," he said, voice soft and slightly amused. "Using your philosophical training against me. I asked the question."

"Alright," Dove soothed, moving close enough so that she could run her fingers through his hair. She'd been wanting to do that all night. Something had held her back. For a man to do that to a woman was one thing, but the other way around felt far more intimate. "I'll answer the question. No, Wes, it doesn't bother me. I don't count age as a good basis for a relationship. Mental maturity and personality are far more important. Frankly, if we were suited, and you were seventy, it wouldn't matter to me."

"You're exaggerating," Wes said, though his shoulders slumped in what looked like relief.

"No," Dove touched her forehead to his. "If I were, do you think I'd have let you kiss me like that?"

"Like what?"

"Like the ground had fallen away from my feet, but it didn't matter, because you were standing right there and would certainly keep me upright." Dove hadn't meant to say all that, but it slipped out. She saw a flash of pleasure cross his eyes and knew that it had been the right thing to say. For all his self-confidence and the fact that he had initiated their intimacy, the age difference between them had bothered him. It was like the film script, she realised with a quiet smirk. Their characters were meant to be overcoming the hurdles that might arise with a disparity in ages, as well as her psychological wounds. He was meant to heal her, and she was meant to love him for it.

Dove wasn't sure about love, but being with Wes that evening had certainly helped push her wariness and fear aside. If she could do something to reassure him, to push away his worries, then she considered it more than an even exchange. Her stress had almost vanished and she felt happy. Not carefree. She doubted that she would ever be carefree, but happy was a good start.

10

The first day of filming was, in a word, overwhelming. Wes had warned Dove about the chaos the day before. They'd been exchanging text messages for a good portion of the day while Dove ran errands, helped Meg by reviewing resumes and packing boxes, did some of the book-keeping for the cafe, and tried her very best not to panic about what Monday held. The text messages from Wes, despite being very clear and helpful, had done next to nothing to prepare her for the first filming day.

She arrived early, as ordered by Charlie and reminded by Marc, twice. She had come holding a cup of tea and yawning at the early hour and barely had time to look around for Wes before she was whisked away by the costume and makeup people. There, she spent nearly three hours making sure everything fit right and the makeup wasn't too much. Given that they were starting with the first scene—where she walked into a police station with blood all over her—it was rather difficult to judge what was too much.

By the time Dove was dressed and made-up, she felt like an entirely different person. Which was the point, she supposed. She wore a filmy summer dress that was far too light for the cold weather. Though the warehouse had heaters, Dove found herself shivering. She forced herself to blame that reaction on the weather, not the fake blood or her nerves. The dress was torn slightly and splattered with fake blood, which was also on any exposed skin. Dove's hair was half-up and more fake blood had been splattered there.

She was then led to the centre of the warehouse's open space, where a street scene and some green screens were set up, cameras and lighting equipment and microphones everywhere. Charlie was waiting for her, talking with Rachel. Wes, despite the fact that he wasn't in the scene, was standing around as well. He caught a glimpse of Dove and turned to face her. Dove felt a surge of pleasure before it vanished. Wes looked at her not with joy, but absolute horror and shock.

"They're certainly thorough in the makeup department," Wes said as she came up. His voice was steady, and the horror had been smoothed away an instant after Dove spotted it, but she swore she saw a flicker there, in his eye. He quickly sipped at his bottle of water. Charlie faced her with scrutiny before nodding. He didn't seem horrified in the slightest.

"Yes, they do. It's perfect. Now, let's get started

filming before the blood dries," Charlie said. He waved his hands and the camera crew got into their places. Dove felt absolutely ridiculous and did her best to ignore the looks she got from the various people, but their shock was disconcerting. Rachel, at least, gave her a friendly look before vanishing into the "police station." Dove was handed a knife—also spotted with blood—and Charlie placed her in the appropriate spot.

Dove glanced at Wes once to be sure that she was doing things correctly. "Okay, love, just remember, you're Casey. You've just been attacked, and you barely got away with your life. You've also just killed a man. You're in shock. Okay? Go for it."

Dove swallowed, her mind retreating into itself at Charlie's words. *Attacked.* Fear and panic set their fangs into her and she knew that she was about to have a panic attack. There was nothing she could do to prevent this. None of her coping techniques would work just then; she was too far into the depths of panic. It was already in her mind, rearing its ugly head and taking over. She wasn't sure where the strength to do as she was directed by Charlie came from, but she did as she was bade. Dove was barely aware of her moving across the set, holding the knife out at a dangerous angle, breathing heavily. She stumbled towards the facade of the building that Rachel was in and, as directed, fell against the door, slipping inside.

Everyone in the "station" started in shock and Dove tried to remember, in the back of her mind, whether or not this was real. Someone's arms caught her before she could fall to the ground and Dove was vaguely aware of Rachel speaking in her ear. She knew that she had to speak, had a line to say, but the words came out slurred.

"What's that?" Rachel asked, taking the knife from Dove. Dove half-expected Charlie to stop them, make her do it all over again because of her mistake, but he didn't. So she spoke again, pushing herself to enunciate.

"I t-think h-he's dead," she said, her breath catching in her throat. Dove made a sound. "H-he attacked m-me and, uh, and then..." she gestured to the knife that Rachel held before completely breaking down into incoherent sounds. Rachel, true to her character, called out for someone to help her.

"Cut!" Charlie's voice broke through the haze that covered Dove's mind. She grabbed onto it like a lifeline, realising that it wasn't real. She was okay. She was safe. Her body was less quick to give up the fantasy, but she at least managed enough coherence to stand and stagger off past the cameras and into the loo. She dry-heaved twice before her entire breakfast came up and then Dove just knelt there, feeling dizzy. She shouldn't have been surprised when someone knocked on the door.

"Dove?" Wes knocked again. She didn't feel much like moving or talking and just sat there. The panic was subsiding as she regained her foothold on reality, but her entire body was shaking. She had probably ruined the makeup that the artists had spent so much time on. "Dove," Wes said again, his voice clearer. Dove looked up and saw that he was in the room with her, looking on in concern. She must not have locked the door.

"It'll be alright," Dove said. She ignored Wes' look of disbelief and instead held up her hand to gauge how badly she was shaking, how long it would take her to recover. Pretty badly. Wes grabbed her hand and kept it steady.

"Come on, Dove, you're a mess. And I'm not talking about the fake blood," he said, brushing a strand of sticky hair out of her eyes. Dove swallowed and focused on the sensation, glad for the contact of someone who cared. "What's going on?"

"It'll be fine," Dove echoed her earlier statement. "It happens. And it will go away."

"What is it? Some sort of morning sickness?"

Dove laughed outright at the idea, the sound dry and harsh. She shook her head. "No. Nothing like that."

"Then what? You're worrying me. Not to mention Charlie. Everyone." Wes peered into her eyes, his searching gaze trying to catch an idea of whatever it was that was bothering her. Dove replied with a half-smile. He cared, obviously, but it was nice to be able to bask in that for a moment. It had been so rare in her life.

"Panic attacks," Dove murmured. She didn't want to go into details, especially not about *why* she had panic attacks, and so hoped that he would just accept her words. He may have cared, but like other people, dealing with her emotional baggage was often too much. Dove didn't want to ruin whatever this was before she got a chance to figure it out.

"I'm sorry," Wes put his hand on her shoulder, squeezing it gently. Dove shrugged.

"They don't happen all the time, but I think the smell of the fake blood must have set me off," she lied softly. Wes nodded in understanding. "They probably want me to do another take, huh?" Dove asked, wanting nothing more than a shower to wash all the makeup off.

"Probably. I think that was fantastic, though," Wes said. Dove shrugged and shook her head.

"You're probably just saying that. I appreciate the effort, though." Dove smiled and stood. She wanted to rinse out her mouth, but feared smearing more of the makeup. She took a deep breath and walked out of the loo, Wes following behind, looking mildly exasperated at the crowd of people waiting for them. Charlie was hovering anxiously, Marc right beside him and looking equally worried.

"Oh, thank goodness," Charlie said, reaching out and pausing just before he touched Dove, eyes taking in the fake blood. "I thought that something had happened to you!"

"Sorry," Dove apologised emphatically, swallowing down the knowledge that this was likely to happen again. "I think the smell of the blood set me off."

"I didn't even think to ask if you were allergic to

makeup," Charlie said. He glanced at Marc, who pulled out his phone and wrote something down. "But that's okay. I want to do one more take. It isn't really necessary, but we can change up the angles and get some extra shots for editing. Oh the whole, that was great. You're a natural."

Dove blinked. A compliment from Wes or Charlie alone was one thing, but from both? It seemed too farfetched to be a conspiracy between them to make her calmer. So she allowed herself a small smile and murmured thanks. Then, after being almost assaulted by the makeup crew to be certain she hadn't ruined anything, Dove walked back on the set.

The cameras adjusted and one of the technicians did something with the lights and there was some rearrangement of people. Charlie gave the indication to start again and once more, Dove stepped into that dark part of her mind. It wasn't as bad, this time around, because she knew that she had done this before and that it would be over in a few minutes. Despite her self-assurances, the pounding of her heart got louder and louder and by the time she collapsed into Rachel's arms, she wasn't entirely faking the faint.

"Cut!" Charlie called again. "Dove, darling, that was great. Now go get that blood off of you before I have to send you to hospital."

"Everything alright?" Rachel asked quietly. "I know this can be overwhelming and you've never done this before. Do you want me to ask for a break for the day? Charlie will do it if I make him."

"Thank you," Dove said, "but I think a quick shower and something to eat and I'll be okay."

Rachel nodded, but she didn't look convinced. Dove made her escape before any further questions could be asked. She went to the only place in the warehouse she had any peace—her dressing room. Dove managed to close the door behind her, strip off her clothes and get into the shower before she started crying from shame.

11

—————

*D*ove made it back to her flat at the end of the day completely exhausted. Who knew that filming was quite so intensive? Makeup, costumes, shooting multiple takes with different lighting, camera angles, styles of interaction and whatever else Charlie decided to throw her way left her stunned and slightly dazed, not entirely sure what happened. And that wasn't taking into account the panic attack.

She had done only one more scene—that with Rachel at a coffee shop—but it had taken a good portion of the rest of the day. Wes had been whisked away for his own scenes, mostly one with Roman that introduced the character of Vaughn. He, like Rachel and Dove, hadn't even finished the scene before Charlie threw up his hands and called it a day. Both Dove and Wes imagined that the end of the day was done by Marc's prompting rather than Charlie's exasperation. Certainly, the assistant was still watching her with a measured amount of concern.

Wes had mentioned a quick trip to a chips shop, but Dove took one look at the weariness he was wearing, not to mention her own aches and pains, before deciding that she should just go home. She had kissed Wes on the cheek and somehow come away feeling almost as woozy as the first kiss had made her. That was enough to smooth out any remaining ruffled feathers from that morning.

W: *Are you at your flat yet?*

Wes texted Dove. She was touched by his concern to make certain she arrived home safely. If he were anyone else, she would be slightly annoyed by the fact that he didn't think she could take care of herself. With Wes, though, it just made him a gentleman.

D: *Just got home. Next up: a hot bath.*

Dove leaned against her door as she typed out the message. She took a deep breath and felt her muscles aching slightly. She hadn't even done anything physically demanding and yet she was sore. Well, excepting throwing up her breakfast. That was likely enough to explain everything. Mostly.

"Dove? Is that you?"

Dove jerked up from her position against the door and reached into her purse for the item she always kept close at hand, even when she sometimes forgot her wallet or phone: pepper spray, the legal kind. It wasn't particularly effective as a weapon, but as a deterrent to give her the chance to escape, it worked perfectly well. She lifted the canister and prepared to spray her attacker, adrenaline making the aches vanish.

A man rounded the corner from the kitchen, holding a plate with some toast on it, looking dishevelled and tired. Dove tensed before relaxing. "Peter," she breathed in relief.

The man frowned at Dove and gestured to the canister with a piece of toast. "You weren't really going to spray me with that, were you?" he asked. "You wouldn't do such a thing to your brother, would you?"

"If you deserved it, yes," Dove said without remorse, a twitch at the corner of her mouth hiding her wry smile. She put the canister away in her purse and took a long look at her brother. He was tall and lanky with a golden tan that came from spending a lot of time outdoors in tropical places. His hair was usually the same colour as Dove's chestnut, but the sun had lightened it a few shades to almost a light brown. It hung around his face and framed the sharp features that were so unlike Dove's slightly rounded ones. He wore a long pair of khaki trousers and a button-up linen shirt with a tattered cardigan over top. He looked tired—evident in the dark circles under his eyes—and underfed, but other than that he was Dove's brother through and through.

"Well, do I pass the inspection?" Peter asked, stuffing the last of the toast in his mouth with the same manners as a three-year-old. Dove stepped forwards and wrapped her arms around him, pleased with his solid hug in return.

"Where have you been?" Dove asked, though she was careful to keep the reproach out of her voice. That would get her absolutely nowhere. She looked up at him. "Thailand, last I heard, but that was a month ago."

"Singapore," Peter replied. "There was this guy who said he could use an English speaker in Singapore for a while, so there I went. Of course, as soon as I saw a picture of my baby sister standing inches away from Weston Blackwood and looking far too comfortable, there was nothing to do but return home."

Dove bit her lip and lowered her gaze. She pulled away from her brother's hug and gathered her purse, stowing the pepper spray back inside. She moved farther into her flat and set her purse on the kitchen counter before sinking into one of the chairs at the table. "You saw that?" she asked.

"So you're not denying that it was Weston Blackwood." Peter sat across from Dove, his gaze hardening slightly. The note of incredulity in his voice stung. Dove shook her head.

"No," she answered. "That was him."

"I'm not sure I even want to know how you got mixed up in something involving a man like him. The fact that you did and you're not running far away from it is, frankly, astonishing, Dove," Peter growled lowly. He put his hands on the table and interlaced his fingers, exactly the way a scolding parent would a young child.

"I work with him," Dove explained. "A man came to the cafe last week and wanted to hire me to be in his film."

"You got hired to be an actress in some film? Bullshit," Peter said. Dove winced. "Now how did this really happen? Did the man come to the cafe and decide to ask you out? Did he think that slumming was going to get him some easy sex? Having as much money and fame as he does, it ought to be easy for him."

"Slumming?" Dove spat the offending word out. Peter nodded, his expression grim. "Is that what you think is happening?"

"What else could it possibly be, Dove? The man is what, fifteen, twenty years older than you? Men that age don't go around with younger women because they like the conversation." Peter flattened his hands on the table and stood, looming over Dove. "I don't care what you think, I don't want this continuing. Fame and money are tempting and addictive, Dove, but they mean *nothing*. Do you even know about this man's past?"

"Does it matter?" Dove said quietly, though she knew that Peter would think it did and wasn't surprised when he curled his lip and shook his head.

"Of course it matters." He sat down again and stared at her. "Take it from me. I've travelled all over the world and met lots of people. Knowing about their past would have helped me get out of a few scrapes. This guy has a lot more clout than a wanderer like me. His past is going to hold a lot darker things than an angry ex."

"Oh? Like what? He's actually a really nice person," Dove argued. She was feeling as though this attack against Wes was an attack against her. It was unreasonable, she tried to tell herself. She should be listening to her brother and not her feelings for Wes. She hardly knew Wes. But she didn't believe what Peter was telling her and she didn't want to. As far as she was concerned, Wes was a good person. He dispelled her panic attacks, not caused them. That was good enough for her.

"Think about it. That lifestyle leads to a lot of drugs and alcohol and sex. Things you shouldn't be getting mixed up in. You're not an actress, Dove, you run a cafe. Just stick to your own, alright?" Peter reached out to grab her hand. Dove pulled away, not bothering to hide the hurt in her eyes.

"You know, as my brother, you should believe me about these things," Dove murmured. "If not about the man, then about my life. It turns out, Peter, that I am an actress. I was hired by Charles Wash to feature in his next film. I've hired someone to run the cafe in my absence. I've met great people and I don't care that Wes is rich or famous or older than I am. He's nice and doesn't care that I've got nothing but a cafe that I didn't even want to my name. Not everyone cares about money, and you know I would never get involved in drugs or worthless sex. I've only known him a week. I'm not as corruptible as you seem to think. You could have a little faith in me."

She shoved her chair back from the table and snatched her purse off the counter, wiping at her eyes with the back of her hand. If she expected Peter to call after her, she would have been disappointed, but Dove wanted him to just leave her alone. She went to her room and pulled out a weekend bag, stuffing some pyjamas inside and grabbing her toothbrush and whatever else she might need. Then she stalked out, stopping by the kitchen for half a moment, her anger showing through her teary eyes. Peter hadn't moved, his arms folded and his expression halfway to a sneer.

"You can stay the night, but tomorrow Meg and her son are moving in, so you'll have to be gone. Call me when you decide that you'd rather believe me than attack my decisions," Dove said. She turned and practically ran out the door. Her brother did not call after her; not that she had expected him to.

It was dark, and she knew that she probably shouldn't be walking around at night, but Dove was gladder for the darkness to hide her tears than she was afraid. She made it to the warehouse and her dressing room before she collapsed completely. She was a mess, laying on her couch and trying to control the sobs that wracked her entire body. Had Peter come back from Singapore just to yell at her for making poor decisions? He had been gone for years, communicating only by email and social media and maybe a call at the holidays, and the only thing he had to say was that she was being a fool? Dove thought family was meant to stand by you and support you when no one else would. Maybe that was friends. Maybe it wasn't anyone at all.

She loved Peter, desperately. But she realised that she did not like him much. At the moment, she was just glad that they only shared a mother. It meant she could hold on to the distance between them as something genetic, something completely beyond her control. It meant she could pretend that there was nothing she could do about the distance between them.

W: *Enjoying the bath?*

Dove nearly started crying again at the text from Wes. It was meant to be teasing and suggestive, but all she saw was someone who actually liked her and was willing to talk.

Back at the warehouse, Dove texted in response, blowing her nose with some bath tissue.

W: *What? Why?*

The response was immediate and Dove could feel the concern radiating from those two words. See, she wanted to shout at Peter. He cares. He's not just using me.

D: *Long story. Think I'll stay the night.*

W: *I'll be there in ten minutes. You can tell me then. Should I bring something to drink?*

Dove bit her lip.

D: *That sounds perfect. Thank you.*

W: *Anytime.*

12

———

This all felt too familiar. Wes was experiencing some serious deja vu, and he wasn't quite sure what to think. The late-night conversations, the meeting at the empty studio to talk and do who knows what else, it was all something he had done before. This time was different. Felt different. Or at least, he tried to tell himself that.

The truth was, he liked Dove. A lot more than he had liked any of the actresses he had previously worked with. That was the problem, though. He *liked* Dove. It had nothing—not much, at least—to do with the fact that Wash had asked him to seduce her and make her more comfortable. No, Wes figured he would have gravitated towards Dove no matter what. The issue was that he wasn't some innocent man coming straight out an ideal idea of life with a romanticised view of the world. He was dark and cynical and he didn't trust what every instinct was screaming at him: that Dove was special.

Whenever Wes was with Dove, those thoughts won out. It was afterwards, in the quiet of his own flat, that he began to doubt. He was sure he was heading straight into a bad situation. Again. Yet here he was, standing outside Dove's dressing room, holding a box of chocolates in one hand and a bottle of wine in the other. He knocked.

Dove opened the door and her face lit up when she saw him. The mere action made all of Wes' doubts vanish and he held up the bottle of wine. "I hope you have glasses."

"I have a mug." Dove stepped aside to let him in. "Sorry."

"That's alright. We'll share." Wes smiled. He knew he could have slipped next door to his own room and fished out a pair of tumblers he kept on hand to help his sanity during the filming process, but sharing a wine glass—mug—was far more intimate. The ache in his stomach told him he wanted intimate, no matter the consequences.

Wes settled on the floor and Dove sat next to him, holding out the mug. He poured and let her take the first sip. "Thank you for this," Dove murmured, leaning back against her couch.

"What are you doing back here?" Wes asked. "I thought you'd be enjoying a quiet night getting rid of aches and sores."

"My brother showed up," Dove said simply, a slight

sigh in her voice. Wes blinked. She had a brother? He shouldn't have been surprised, but Dove never came with a family in his mind. She was just independent and alone, strong and needing nothing from anyone. Dove must have caught his shock, because she took a deep sip of the wine before handing the mug to Wes. "Half brother, really."

"Father or mother?" Wes asked. He drank and revelled in the fact that the wine was flavoured from where Dove's lips touched the mug. Silently, he wondered at this ridiculous, cheesy line of thought. He was going to start breaking out into song at any moment. Or worse, producing spontaneous poetry. The thought had him smirking just a little.

"Mother. He's older than I am. His father died and our mother married my father. She died soon afterwards. Car accident," Dove said. Her voice offered no sorrow, so Wes gathered the wound was long since healed.

"So your brother..." Wes said.

"Peter," Dove supplied.

"Peter. Right. I take it you two don't see each other often? Or don't get along?" If it were anyone else, Wes wouldn't bother asking. He didn't care. This was Dove, though. Despite his attempts to the contrary, he seemed to care about her.

"Peter travels a lot. He goes from place to place, doing odd jobs here and there, leaving if someone offers him something more interesting or if he gets bored. He never makes enough to be staying in resort hotels, but the lifestyle seems to suit him and he does well enough. We talk over email or social media every now and again, and we always talk at the holidays, but most of the time we don't talk," Dove explained. She lifted the lid on the box of chocolates and looked at the offerings before putting the lid back down. Now, Wes was worried.

"You don't get along," Wes commented. Dove shrugged, her muscles tensing and relaxing with the movement.

"It's not that we don't get along, it's…" she broke off and pulled her knees to her chest, burying her face between them. She took a deep breath and Wes set his hand on her back. The urge to comfort her and make all of her problems go away was much stronger than his fear of whatever emotion it was that had him tethered to her. Dove looked up at him and Wes nearly staggered with the depth of her emotion in her eyes. It was fathomless, so intense that a casual observer would have thought that it didn't exist. He was far from a casual observer. "It's a long story," Dove murmured, resting her chin on her knees. "I don't want to bore you with the details."

"You could never bore me," Wes said, brushing back some of her hair. He meant it, he realised.

"I imagine if I started reading Aristotle to you, you would be bored. And don't even get me started on Thomas Aquinas." Dove attempted a joke and Wes smiled, if only to make her feel better.

"Alright, barring dead philosophers' written works,

you could never bore me," he acknowledged. "Dove, what is it? I want to know."

"The picture that girl took of us made it onto the internet," Dove whispered. Wes felt as though he were missing half the story. Anger and guilt rose through him. He stifled a low growl, knowing he should have done something about that girl. "Peter saw it and came home to warn me off of you. I tried to explain that we were working together and that this wasn't about—" she broke off and bit her lip.

Wes finished her sentence for her, knowing precisely what her brother was thinking. It was what most of the world thought. "The sex. He thinks that it's about the sex for me and the fame for you? Because I'm an actor or because I'm older than you are?"

"Both," Dove said quietly. She lifted the lid off the chocolates again and ate one. A weight lifted from Wes and he allowed himself to think that this might be a fixable problem. In his experience, women didn't eat chocolate for two reasons: one, they didn't want to gain weight or were allergic; two, they were upset beyond words. "I gave him all the evidence I had and he still bit my head off."

"It's your life, Dove." Wes draped an arm around her shoulders and pulled her against him. She relaxed further. "You don't need to listen to him. You're capable and intelligent and beautiful."

"I've managed," Dove said. Close enough, Wes figured. "But Peter is family and he thinks that it's wildly inappropriate for me to be with you, let alone acting in a film. If he had his way, I would never leave the cafe again."

"Family always manages to get under your skin," Wes agreed. "It's a special skill."

Dove scoffed, but there was a slight smile to her expression. "I don't want to stop," she admitted. "The acting or whatever *this* is."

"This? You mean sitting around drinking wine and eating chocolate with an old man?" Wes filled the mug with wine and offered it to Dove. She shook her head and he set it aside.

"Old man?" she murmured. Or purred, Wes realised belatedly as she turned and fixed him with the most breathtaking, seductive smile he had ever seen. Her eyes were half-lidded and the tip of her tongue flicked out to wet her lips. Wes' heartbeat went straight to the place between his legs and he swallowed. "I prefer the term mature. Experienced. Wise," she breathed the last word and leaned up to capture his lips.

He wanted to devour her. Some semblance of self-control remained, though, and he managed to keep his hands to himself, instead focusing on the taste of wine and chocolate and Dove. She pulled back a moment later and looked at him, as if asking if he were alright. "Wise," Wes choked out. "I don't think there's much wisdom about me."

"Not from where I'm sitting," Dove replied. Wes chuckled and kissed her again, taking her bottom lip between his teeth. Dove made a sound in the back of her throat and Wes grinned. There was something satisfying about enticing a woman make those sounds.

"I know some people who would disagree with you," Wes murmured, pushing forwards until Dove was moving backwards and he was on his knees. "But if you insist."

"Wes," Dove said, her eyes widening. He cocked his head and smiled, a surge of pleasure making it quite clear to him that he was exactly where he wanted to be. He reached out and pulled his fingers through Dove's waves of hair, revelling in the feeling. He wanted to see her beneath him, that hair spread out and wild as he made her call his name.

Wes pushed in again for a kiss and Dove retreated, making another sound. This wasn't happy, like it had been, this was panicked and terrified. Wes pulled back.

"Dove?" he asked. She was backed into a corner, her eyes wide, not with pleasure but fear. Her breathing was heavy and she kept clenching and unclenching her fists. He had only seen the beginnings of it, but it wasn't hard to recognise; Dove was having a panic attack. "Dove, it's okay," Wes said, holding up his hands.

What could have set it off? She wasn't stressed from the filming. That was over for the day. And the issue with her brother had obviously made her upset, but nothing worse than typical family annoyance. She had initiated the kiss, he had pushed forwards and—Wes blanched, cursed, and moved away from Dove, feeling like the biggest bastard in the world.

"crap," he said. "Dove, I'm sorry. I'm so sorry. I didn't know."

She looked away, her eyes filled with shame. Her breathing was calming, but the panic was still on her face. It was like a knife in Wes' chest, each time she clenched her fists. He liked Dove, that much was obvious. She liked him too, apparently. He figured they could get over the issue of age and his fame meant nothing to her. But this? He wasn't sure how to deal with this. But he still wanted, more than anything at that moment, to comfort her, to make her understand that everything would be alright.

"Why didn't you tell me?" Wes whispered, putting even more distance between them. "That you were..."

Dove lifted her eyes and the pain was obvious. The sadness suddenly made sense, as did her closed-off nature. He swallowed, his tongue dry at the thought of bringing it up into the open. Dove didn't have the same qualms, though, because she finished his sentence.

"Raped," she said. "I was raped."

___

a small part of Wes whispered, *See? This is why you shouldn't have got invested in the girl. You don't need the baggage. What are you meant to do with that? Let her cry on your shoulder?* Another, more dominant part of him was merely horrified and sympathetic, wanting to do whatever it was that would make her feel better. The problem was, Wes had no idea how to solve Dove's problem, or even make her more comfortable. His initial instinct was to pull her to him and wrap his arms around her, but under the circumstances, that was unlikely to be a good plan.

"I..." he trailed off. There was nothing to say. Nothing that he thought would help, in any case. "I'm sorry," was all he could settle for. Dove replied by laughing drily. It was dark and cynical and the most depressing thing Wes had ever heard coming from her throat.

"It wasn't your fault," she said. "I was the one foolish enough to walk into the situation."

"I merely meant to express sympathy," Wes breathed. Dove nodded and rubbed her eyes with her hand. "Dove, please..." he trailed off again, this time because he was afraid she would turn away from him. Pulling away in the midst of a panic attack, that he could understand. But turning away when all he wanted to do was offer his support, that would be too painful.

"I went to a concert with some friends from university," Dove narrated. Wes wanted to close his eyes and block his ears. He didn't want to hear this. But Dove had lived through it and he owed her to listen. "They wanted to go out clubbing afterwards. I had an exam to study for, so I went back to campus. To the library."

"Dove," Wes choked out. She shook her head, her hair flying loose in strands around her face.

"Please let me tell this," she said. "I need this."

Wes swallowed back a retort that no, she didn't, and simply nodded. "Alright," he said.

"I was studying psychology at the time, planning on doing my best to get out of the cafe and move on to greater things. I wanted to... I don't know. It doesn't matter. All that matters is that I went back to study and go over some articles for the exam. And one of my professors was there. He offered to help me get through some of the more dense material and I accepted. We went back to his office and... he closed the door and raped me. Demanded that I tell no one, or my grades would suffer and I would never get my degree. Afterwards, he just said that I was sure to do well on the exam." Dove shuddered, the tremor moving through her entire body. Wes felt ill, bile rising in the back of his throat. He wanted to hug her and simultaneously go kill the man who had done this to her. It was someone she had trusted, too. He said nothing, not trusting himself to speak.

"I changed my degree." Dove picked at some imaginary lint on her trousers and flicked it away, as if that were the most important thing right then. "It wasn't easy—surely you know how little they like you changing things, especially near the end of the first year. But I finally broke down in the middle of the administrator's office and said why. I had to submit a report—anonymous, of course—and the police investigated. He was arrested and I studied philosophy instead."

"Why philosophy?" It was the only thing Wes could think to ask. He had asked it before, but now the answer seemed to matter more. Much more.

"Because it was easier thinking about the collective minds of humanity than what could have gone on inside a single man's head." Dove wiped her eyes again. More tears slipped down her cheeks despite her efforts. Wes reached out and brushed his thumb over one of the droplets, making Dove smile slightly. It was weak, but at least it was there.

"I'm sorry," Wes said again, moving to sit next to her. He didn't touch her again, even though he wanted to offer whatever comfort he could. He just sat close and made sure that she knew he was there.

"I know," Dove murmured. "And I'm sorry, too."

"For what? You have nothing to be sorry about."

"Not apologising. Expressing... no, I am apologising." Dove leaned her head against Wes' shoulder. "I'm sorry for these panic attacks. I can't control them. But they're not as bad as they were. Around you, I mean."

"Like when I brushed your cheek at the reading and you ran?" Wes felt understanding dawn on him. Dove nodded.

"But I got over it," she said. "It just takes some time and convincing my brain that you're not going to hurt me."

"I would never hurt you," Wes assured her. She nodded.

"I know. My subconscious is constantly looking for threats, though. That's what we have to convince." Dove looked up at him. The look in her eyes made the anger flare up and Wes wanted nothing more than to beat on the man who had done this. He was glad the bastard was in prison, but that didn't change his protective instincts. Who would have thought? Him. Protective. Of *her*. He was getting in way over his head, Wes knew. This was moving past dangerous territory and was impossible to fight, now. That niggling feeling in the back of his mind that was telling him to get out before his emotional attachment got too strong was being ground into dust.

Wes may have agreed to get close to Dove to please

Wash and clear the debt between them; that wasn't the reason why he was sitting next to her right then. That was something entirely different.

"I didn't want to drag you into my mess," Dove sighed. "Between Peter and the issues in my past, you have just been hit with practically all of my emotional problems. You have enough to deal with, I'm certain."

"Dove, there's no reason to be sorry. I'm not in this relationship to avoid anything more difficult than a spilled cup of coffee," Wes said, realising that he had just defined whatever he had with Dove as a relationship. So much for ambiguity. "If I wanted nothing deeper than what sales are on at Tesco, then I would be dating someone far less interesting and intelligent, not to mention far more self-involved and basically ignorant of the world. What happened to you was terrible. That doesn't mean I don't want to share the burden."

Truth, he realised. All of it. There was no more lying to her. And that would mean telling her about his past. Sharing his burdens. Not tonight, though, he decided as Dove moved closer, lifting his arm around her shoulders. No, there was enough pain tonight.

"So," Wes said. "Do you want some more wine, or would that just make things worse?"

Dove laughed and nodded. "Some wine sounds wonderful."

They drank and ate some more of the chocolate for a while, not really talking but just sitting there. Wes wasn't sure how to talk about anything less serious than their previous conversation at the moment. If it were a different day, then maybe things would be easier, but the confession was too heavy on his mind. Luckily for him, Dove had lived with the experience longer.

"What now?" she asked at the end of their second mug of wine. "Everything feels different."

"Does it? Sure, I'll be a bit more cautious with you, more patient, but it doesn't change how I think about you. Or how I feel about you." Wes bit into a chocolate and cursed his personal trainer for having him on such a restrictive diet. He was going to get a serious scolding for the indulgence.

"So, what, we just continue on as before?" Dove scoffed. Wes shrugged.

"Why not?" he asked. "I told you. You're capable and independent and beautiful. This doesn't change that. Actually, the fact that you've become all of that in spite of what happened is sort of fantastic."

"Thank you," Dove murmured. She stretched and sighed, leaning back against the couch. With the heel of her foot, she kicked her phone away. "I imagine Peter is going to kill me tomorrow."

Wes grabbed the change of topic with something between relief and sorrow. Relieved because they could get back to normal, whatever that was. Sorry because the depth of connection that had existed between them for a moment was fading into something more superficial. "Why?"

"I may have yelled at him and then told him he had to be out of my flat by tomorrow so Meg can move in.

It's not that I don't love him, but I have no idea how to get him to believe me. And if he doesn't want to believe me, then I have no idea how we can possibly... you know," Dove said. Her voice was dropping off slowly. Wes looked at her—really looked—and cursed himself for not seeing how tired she was. She had been exhausted after finishing filming. This situation with her brother and with him probably hadn't helped. He remembered countless first days and the exhaustion that inevitably followed. She needed a good sleep.

"You could invite him to the warehouse. Have Wash go at him," Wes suggested.

Dove chuckled, her eyes drooping. "I would enjoy that," she murmured. "Hey, Wes?"

"Hmm?" he put his arm around her shoulder again and gently pulled her into him, offering a place to rest.

"Thanks. And please don't tell anyone," she said.

"Wouldn't dream of it." Wes kissed the top of Dove's head, breathing in her scent. She murmured something else and then her breathing slowed and smoothed out. A moment later, she was asleep. Wes followed not long after.

14

───────

ove woke with a crick in her neck. She groaned quietly and lifted her head, stretching her shoulders at the same time. Her neck popped and she froze, squeezing her eyes against the pain. "Ow," she squeaked. A moment later and the discomfort dissipated. Dove sat up fully and found that the reason she had a kink in her neck was because she had slept on her couch, using Wes as a pillow. She remembered, vaguely, falling asleep on him after they finished the bottle of wine, and then being moved to the couch, but it was hazy enough that it might have been a dream. Still, as nice as it was waking up to Wes' handsome face, Dove was feeling sore. Some of it had carried through from her work the day before.

"Right," she murmured, searching around for her phone while she rubbed her eyes. She spotted it on the floor by the small vanity and groaned. She shuffled over to the device and clicked the screen on. Then, she winced. Three calls from Peter, as well as numerous text messages. Not to mention it was barely five in the morning.

"Dove?" Wes sounded as groggy as Dove was feeling. She turned and looked at him through a curtain of her hair. He was really quite handsome, she decided, biting her bottom lip. With his morning stubble and dark hair tousled into disarray, he looked so real. He was someone you could wake up beside, not the untouchable idol that others seemed to believe he was. Though, she had never seen him that way. He had always been real to her, if unreasonably handsome. "What's going on?"

"Nothing," Dove assured him. "I just... I need to take a shower and get dressed. I think I put some clothes in my travel bag."

"What time is it?" Wes stretched and sat up, his shirt wrinkled from having been slept in. She felt badly for keeping him there all night, but she had fallen asleep and couldn't be responsible for what he did after that. Dove supposed that he had chosen to stay. A warm feeling spread right beneath her collar bone and she rubbed the spot absently.

"Early. Fiveish." Dove looked through her bag and let her shoulders slump in relief. She had packed clothes. She wouldn't have to go back to her flat and risk running into Peter. Had he even bothered to stay or given up on her as a lost cause? Dove wouldn't have been surprised if he had just stayed at a hotel, not wanting to spend the night in a place where his fallen sister was living. Then, she had planned on inviting him to the set today, as Wes suggested, to get everything cleared up. It wasn't that she didn't love her brother, but she wasn't feeling all that inclined to interact with him.

"Okay." Wes murmured, rolling his shoulders. "I'll go to my dressing room and take a shower, too. Then we can go out for breakfast before we have to come back for work."

Dove nodded absently. She slipped into her personal bathroom and turned on the water, staring at herself in the mirror as she rubbed her sore neck and shoulders. There was a smudge of chocolate on her cheek and she was feeling the start of a headache coming on. Probably the result of drinking wine and no water. Or maybe just thinking about her brother coming to voice his opinions to Charlie was getting her nervous.

It had nothing to do with the fact that Wes knew all about her secret. Dove shook her head and turned away from her reflection, stepping into the shower. He had said that he didn't care, that he was impressed with her. He had called her beautiful and let her sleep in his arms. There was still a niggling feeling in the back of her mind that left Dove unsettled and uncertain. She had held onto this for so long that it was difficult having it out in the open. She feared the judgement that people would hold, positive or negative.

She wasn't some sort of person to be praised for

having survived such an event. There was no choice in that matter. Nor did she want the pity of people who saw her as a victim. Perhaps that was why she had never told Peter or her father. Her father. Dove rinsed the conditioner out of her hair and winced. He had gone to his grave never understanding why she had given up a promising degree in psychology for something as useless as philosophy. Why she had changed from ambitious and cheerful to silent and content to do nothing more than work at the cafe. Was that why she was working in the film?

"Enough already," Dove said. She turned the water off and dressed, purposefully turning her mind away from that line of thinking. Once she started down that path, there was going to be trouble. So she thought about what to do with her hair to impress Wes. And she thought about what to have for breakfast and what scene Charlie would want to work on today. She scoffed and shook her head. Pushing unpleasant ruminations aside had become rather a specialty of hers. Did that show a presence of mind and a determination to be optimistic? Or was she merely a fool?

Wes pushed the cracked door open a bit and stuck his head in, eyes respectfully closed. "Door was open," he said. "Are you ready?" Dove silently thanked him for the intrusion and rose, wrapping an old cardigan around her.

"Yes," she said. "It's still early, though. I don't know where we're going to find anything to eat."

"Surely one of the cafes has to be open for those

people going to work early in the morning." Wes held out his arm for her to take, which Dove did happily, pulling herself close to him and enjoying the contact.

"I don't imagine there are all that many people going in to work at—" she checked the time on her phone, "five forty-five in the morning."

"You're probably right," Wes rubbed his neck. "Well, I very much doubt the kitchen here has any decent food. It's too early in the process for that." Dove furrowed her brows and he continued. "People tend to bring in food and supplies for making decent meals when they figure out how much time they'll be spending here. It usually takes about a month or so. Which means that there won't be anything but cold coffee drinks and maybe some bottled water."

"You make it sound as though we're going to be living here," Dove murmured, looking at the tall ceilings of the warehouse. Wes laughed drily.

"Last night was not some anomaly. It happens all the time. We're just part of the few people that actually have a separate room for ourselves. I would expect to share your bathroom at some point." Dove made a face and Wes laughed again, this time sincerely. "I wouldn't worry too much. We actors are a polite bunch when it comes to asking for sleeping space. We're too used to luxury not to. Anyways, I don't know anything else to do about breakfast except take you back to my flat. I went to the market a few days ago, so there should still be something in the fridge."

Dove was certain she was blushing. She lifted a

hand to touch her cheek and sure enough, it was warm. She cursed her proclivity towards blushing and hoped desperately that Wes would look away. As he was currently focused on going down the stairs, it seemed likely. "I was going to say we could stop at a market, but that would rather ruin the point, wouldn't it?" Dove said. She stumbled on the last stair—exhaustion and embarrassment were never a good combination—and found herself steadied by Wes. Who had very capable hands. She imagined them brushing against her naked skin and a surge of panic reared through her, overwhelming the lust.

Wes must have seen her momentary fear because he let her go as soon as she was steady on her feet. Dove murmured an apology, mortified. "Don't apologise," Wes soothed. Dove accepted his arm again and focused her attention on the floor. "This isn't your fault."

"No, but I thought I was—we were—doing so well," she hissed furiously. Dove shook her head. "Maybe last night exacerbated things."

"Then we'll go slowly. Start with breakfast. Maybe even move up to lunch at some point," Wes teased. It was kind of him, Dove thought, not to be offended by her reaction. The truth was, she wanted him. She wanted him to kiss her and touch her and evoke pleasure as he brushed his mouth across his skin. The visceral reaction to his touch could prove to be a problem, though. Which was why she was forcibly shoving down panic so frequently. Maybe, Dove bit her lip, she should just have sex with him and get rid of those feelings all together. Kissing him had been startling at first, but she got over that quickly enough. Sex might be the same way.

It also might not be.

"You look lost in space," Wes said. He had his phone out and was calling up one of the cars available through the production company. Dove had hoped they could walk to his flat, but in a city of such a large size, it was unlikely. Now she was curious where he lived. Would his flat be sparse or messy? Dove guessed sparse, but not cold. Just rarely lived in. "What are you thinking?"

She felt herself flush slightly again, having thought of sex and where he lived almost in the same moment. "Nothing important. Just what sort of food you might have in your kitchen."

"Ah, well, I'm not entirely certain. I believe there are some eggs left, but then again, they might not be any good." Dove smiled, her worries slowly dissipating, and went with Wes to his flat, whether or not there was any food to be had. She had her suspicions about the sparse-but-comfortable décor of his flat confirmed and was even pleasantly surprised when there was not only some bread for toasting but a parcel of oranges to eat for breakfast. Wes even had a stash of coffee that he insisted was essential to his survival.

They talked about inconsequential things, like the story behind a mug missing its handle or some tips on dealing with Charlie's more difficult days. Neither

Dove's rape nor her brother were brought up, though she did text Peter with the address to the warehouse and an invitation. She did not bother listening to his voicemail messages, as the texts were enough to indicate his frustration. Then she shoved her phone into her purse and happily ignored it for the rest of breakfast, instead choosing to focus her attention on Wes.

He made her laugh. He was hopeless in the kitchen and Dove eventually had to cut in before he burnt the entire loaf of bread. He had a way of telling a story that made it come to life, which was probably why he was such a good actor. And when she talked, he listen to her. His entire attention was on her, his gaze direct but not penetrating or frightening. He leaned in as though gravitating towards her. Dove found herself doing the same. And when she trailed off into silence, their eyes didn't break away. She just stared, leaning closer.

To his credit, Wes didn't push himself on her. Dove definitely made the first move, pressing her lips against his, before he pushed back. The thoughts of caution that she had floating through her mind vanished. All she could think about was Wes and the way his mouth felt on hers: desperate and a little scared, but warm and electric, too. The way he held her head by gently cupping the back of her neck, her hair trapped between his fingers. The fact that she didn't care that the counter she was leaning over was currently bruising her ribs. All she wanted was to get closer.

That terrified and exhilarated her.

15

$\mathcal{P}$eter walked into the warehouse shortly before their break for lunch. Dove was standing by in full costume and makeup, ready to go on for a short scene between her and Katie, the bartender. Currently, Roman was leaning against the bar, sipping on a gin and tonic—Dove knew it was more tonic than gin—and talking with Katie. Dove was meant to go on and have an awkward but meaningful conversation with Roman about Wes, but Charlie was having Roman and Katie do the first half of the scene over and over again. Apparently neither was really displaying the proper character.

So, when Peter walked into the warehouse, looking wary and slightly angry, Dove noticed. She nearly jumped when Charlie yelled, "Cut!" and looked over her shoulder. The director was rubbing his head as though he had a headache and was talking with Marc. Dove bit her lip in worry; with Charlie out-of-sorts, it was probably not the best time to have her brother on set. He *had* agreed to Peter's visit. Even so.

"Dove," Peter said. Dove jumped again and faced her brother. Her attention had been focused on Charlie and she hadn't heard Peter's approach. Thankfully, Wes was away with costume for the moment, so she could introduce Peter without having to fumble her words with Wes. It certainly didn't help that Peter's anger was growing. "Care to tell me what I'm doing here?"

"Dove, darling, who is this? I don't like visitors on the set." Charlie waved Marc aside and focused on the distraction from Roman and Karen. Both actors looked relieved. Charlie strode up to Peter—shorter by a good foot, and quite a bit rounder, the director was still more intimidating—and gave a dark glare. Peter merely raised his eyebrows and looked at his sister, meaning very, very clear.

"Charlie, this is my brother, Peter." Dove waved her hand weakly between the two men. "You said it was alright for him to visit, given the circumstances." Charlie, to her dismay, didn't greet Peter in his normal effusive and over-the-top fashion. The line between his eyebrows deepened and he pursed his lips thoughtfully. "Peter," Dove continued the second half of the introductions, "this is Charles Wash. My current boss."

"Yes," Charlie said, drawing out the word. "Dove told me that you're upset with her for being seen with Wes Blackwood. That you don't believe she's acting, no, *starring*, in my next film. She asked my permission to prove that she was being honest by bringing you here today. Apparently, our dear Dove would rather avoid an argument with her family."

Peter also deepened his frown. "Do you blame me for having a difficult time believing such a ludicrous story about my sister suddenly becoming an actress?"

"Has she been dishonest in the past?" Charlie countered. Dove wanted to run and hide. She was absolutely mortified and Wes hadn't even been introduced into the situation yet. "Frankly, it doesn't matter to me whether or not you believe your sister. She is an independent adult and a very capable woman and if she chooses to act in this film, then it is her business."

"What sort of person picks a woman out of a cafe, promising everything and taking all she's known away from her?" Peter asked. Dove could see that he was holding a clenched fist by his side. Her brother wasn't a terribly stable person. He travelled when he got bored and stayed friends with someone just as long as the person was interesting to him. She didn't want to think about his temper.

"Peter, leave it," Dove said, putting more force into her words than she had used in a very long time. Years, probably. "This is my decision, my life. And Charlie isn't out to do me harm, okay? He saw an opportunity for him and one for me. Turns out they align."

"Dove, you—"

"No, Peter. Enough," Dove interrupted. "I invited you here to show you what I'm doing with my life. I'm living my life away from that cafe. And you know what? I like it."

"You think this can last?" Peter asked, perilously close to a sneer. Dove inhaled sharply and fought the urge to turn away. She had faced worse. Not by choice, but necessity. Her brother just shook his head. "You changed you life from being a potentially successful psychologist to, what, a cafe owner with a degree in philosophy? And now what are you doing? You don't settle, Dove. And this life is not going to last. So what will you have when this is over?"

"I don't settle," Dove laughed weakly. "From the person who moved around the world, never staying in one place more than six months. I've chosen this life, okay. There's no need to attack me for it. Can't you just be happy for me?"

"Not when pictures of you end up on the internet," Peter hissed. Charlie straightened up as though he'd been shocked.

"Pictures?" he asked, looking at Dove with interest. She opened her mouth to defend herself against whatever it was that Charlie was accusing her of—why did it seem that everyone was against her today—when she felt a presence behind her. Wes laid a hand on her shoulder and Dove closed her mouth.

"Those are my fault, Wash," Wes said. "We were going to bingo and some teenager saw us. Me. Snapped a few pictures on her phone and posted them on the internet."

"Damn," Charlie shook his head. "I had hoped to

keep things quiet for a while longer." He looked up and gave a reassuring smile to Dove. "These things happen, love. It wasn't your fault. Don't worry about it."

"You think this is okay?" Peter snapped. Wes tightened his hold on Dove's shoulder and she leaned into him ever so slightly. Instead of being afraid of his touch, it was more comforting than she would have thought. In fact, just breathing in his scent was enough to make her relax despite the fact that her brother was openly verbally attacking her.

"It's annoying," Wes admitted, "but hardly an issue. No one knows who she is, what's going on. People like to tell stories of stalkers and terrible things that happen—" Dove tensed, images of what that might mean springing to mind. It was an angle she hadn't considered. "—but it's extraordinarily rare. I've been in the business for a long time and have had few issues. Nothing beyond mere annoyances."

"Somehow, that doesn't make this any better." Peter's voice was flat and, as far as Dove was concerned, that could mean only one thing.

"Peter, enough," she said once more. "I'm going to say this again. It's *my* life. *My* choices. I'm going to do this whether you like it or not. And if all you're going to do is be rude, then I would like you to leave."

Peter widened his eyes and stared at Dove in shock. She felt shocked herself. She had never done anything like that. Especially not where family was involved. With Wes at her back, though, she felt as though she could take on the world and win. Peter held up his hands and shrugged, "Fine. I'm just looking out for you. You're making another mistake. Just like you did at university. But it's *your* life. Go ahead and throw it away."

"You know nothing about it," Dove murmured. Peter had stopped listening, though, and was busy looking at the warehouse set up. He shook his head and walked away. With every step he took, Dove felt the gap between them widening. She took a deep breath and held it until he was gone. Then her shoulders slumped and she felt as if reality was rearing its ugly head.

"Are you alright?" Wes asked, loud enough for only Dove to hear.

"We used to be close," she sighed. "When I was a child and our mother was still around. He was older than I was, but he didn't care. We would still talk and spend time together. He taught me how to play football."

"I'm sorry." Wes rubbed her shoulder. Dove shrugged.

"It doesn't matter," she said. She turned to Charlie, who was staring after Peter with a tick in his jaw. "Did you want me to go film? Maybe that would help get the characters right?"

Charlie blinked, confused. Then he nodded and waved to Marc. "Yes, perfect. Round up the people. We're going to do this one more time. All the way through, no stopping. Got it?"

"Yes." Marc rushed off to do as he was told. Charlie

nodded firmly and walked towards the set. Dove followed behind, running over her lines in her head. She was about to walk to the set when Wes stopped her, his hand wrapped gently around her wrist.

"It does matter," he murmured, rubbing the inside of her wrist with his thumb and making her skin shiver. "You matter."

Dove smiled. For the first time in a long time, the sadness went from her eyes and her entire face lit up. She turned away before she could see Wes stagger backwards as if struck. All she knew was that she was exactly where she was meant to be.

16

———

*A*fter that first week, Dove settled into her new life with ease. She quickly adjusted to Charlie's quicksilver moods and found herself enjoying acting more and more. There was drama, as there was wont to be when a group of people—especially actors pretending to be emotionally volatile or snarky or anything else—gathered together. Dove weathered that, too, though some days she returned to her flat wanting nothing more than to soak her troubles away in the bath. That was when she usually got greeted by Timmy wrapping his arms around her legs then running off with a loud laugh before Meg could catch him.

Having people constantly around was both a blessing and something that Dove cursed. She was an introvert, naturally inclined to have time to recharge, but she also loved having Meg and Timmy in her apartment, filling it with life. Still, at the end of the day, she often closed herself into her room and collapsed on her bed, asleep within moments. That is, she did that when she wasn't with Wes.

They spent a considerable amount of time at the warehouse, either in his dressing room or hers. After the third such time, they went out and bought a proper set of glasses and plates so that they wouldn't be eating take away with their fingers or the plastic cutlery dug out of the drawers downstairs. There was also a growing collection of food stuffs gathering in the fridge —as Wes predicted. Most of it was theirs.

They wouldn't do much more than talk or watch the occasional movie. Dove wanted to see Wes' films, but he adamantly refused, saying that he didn't want to relive those moments. They kissed and often found themselves in a tangle of limbs, each breathing heavily, but nothing more than that. Dove wanted more, she thought, but neither the panic in the back of her mind nor Wes would go near such intimacy.

Still, Dove was happy. Happier than she'd been in a while. The farther they got in the filming process, with her story mingling with that of her character Casey's, the more Dove thought she was exactly where she wanted to be. It was as though having a fake psychiatrist made up by screenwriters and Charlie Wash was as good as the real thing. Better, because you didn't often get to date the handsome man who played your psychiatrist. They were about halfway through filming before Charlie called the crew together, pulling Dove away from the makeup people as she was in the middle of having her hair done.

"Well, well, I just wanted to say you have all done a wonderful job so far and I'm pleased with each and every one of you." Charlie clapped his hands together and looked over the gathered people eagerly. Roman groaned and Charlie sighed. "Yes, yes, alright, fine. It's that time again. I've got to get the press involved. Obviously there have been rumours of a Charlie Wash film in production, and naturally the hype about Weston Blackwood being here helps, but this business doesn't run on rumours alone."

"I don't understand," Dove whispered to Wes. He shook his head, a frown on his face. Charlie explained before Wes could get a word in edge-wise.

"I've scheduled a press conference for tomorrow at three. You are all going to be there. And the day afterwards, there are scheduled individual interviews. You know the rules. No giving away the plot any more than I allow, no gossip, no details of where we are or how far away we are from finishing. The press will tear into some of you and the rest they don't know so they'll try to get every titbit of information. Do try to remain inconspicuous for a while. And for goodness' sake, take the company cars for the next two weeks. I don't want any unsuspecting photographs on the underground." Charlie stared all of the people down, including the heads of cameras, lighting and the like. Dove wanted to shrink into herself. She had forgotten that being in a film meant people were going to be watching and wanting to know everything about her. It was one thing coming to the warehouse and acting with a bunch of people she had started to consider her friends. It was another entirely to talk casually with the press for the purposes of having her face on every screen around.

Then something occurred to her and she felt that familiar panic rising up in her. She turned and looked at Wes, wide-eyed. "Every titbit of information?" Dove breathed. Wes stiffened and cursed under his breath.

"There are other people that know about it." It wasn't a question, but Dove nodded anyways. Wes curled his lip and hissed through his teeth, obviously trying to gain control of the situation. Charlie seemed to be done talking and was already turning towards Marc to hash out some details of the press conference. Wes looked at Dove and grabbed hold of her hand, squeezing reassuringly. "Come on," he said, and pulled her towards Charlie.

"Wes, please, we can't tell hi—" Dove breathed under her breath. Wes shook his head and stopped before the director.

"Wash, we need to talk to you," Wes said. Charlie raised his eyebrows and smiled widely at the sight of Dove's hand in Wes'. She didn't quite understand his happiness, but it didn't really matter. Her fear was far too pressing to think about that right then.

"What is it, Wes?" Charlie asked, smirking and putting his hands into his pockets, as if the world wasn't about to come crashing down. Or maybe that was just her, Dove thought.

"We can't use Dove's real name in accordance with the film," Wes said flatly. Charlie blinked and raised his eyebrows, exchanging a glance with the ever-present Marc.

"Why not? She doesn't have a competing contract, or anything that would be affected by the use of her name," Marc said, pulling out his phone and typing something, presumably Dove's name, into Google.

"Wash, just trust me. You do not want her name out there," Wes said, his tone perfectly even and deadly serious. Dove felt a shiver run down her spine. "You don't have to change all of it, just the last name. Or, better yet, just use a completely different name entirely. Lots of people do it. This is show business, after all."

"Yes, but they usually have terrible names," Charlie said. "Dove Graves is a perfectly lovely name. One that could do very well in the press."

"Please," Dove put in. She didn't want to have to tell Charlie about what had happened to her. The thought of telling him wasn't nearly as bad as it had been before she had divulged her secret to Wes. And she trusted Charlie not to spread it around, but there was still that deep-seated need to keep it to herself. To keep people from staring at her as though she weren't who she had been. As though she was only that event. Charlie looked at her and sighed, shaking his head.

"If you weren't such a charming girl, you wouldn't

get away with half of the things you do, love." He reached out to cup her chin gently. He smiled. "Fine. Alright, fine. What are you going to call yourself?"

Dove looked desperately at Wes. This was his idea, not hers, but he was staring at her as though he had no idea. Dove wracked her mind, trying to think of something suitably marketable but not absurd. "Felicia?" she asked. Charlie said nothing for a moment, contemplating her face. He tilted his head first one way then another before looking at Marc with raised eyebrows. Marc merely shrugged.

"Felicia is fine. And last name?" This time, Dove was absolutely at a loss. She wanted to pinch the bridge of her nose but settled for rubbing the back of her neck so she didn't mess up what the makeup crew had been doing for most of the morning. It was meant to be for her first date with Vaughn and they wanted it to be perfect.

"How about Norton? It's not too unusual, so people might not question it. And it makes her relatable. Or Teague?" Marc suggested, his fingers once again typing furiously on his phone.

"Teague. Felicia Teague," Charlie tested the name on his tongue and nodded. "It will do. You'd better not change your mind, because this is going to be your name for the rest of your film career."

As Dove hadn't planned to have a career in film, she just nodded and silently thanked Wes for his quick action. The results of having her real name out in the world could have been disastrous. There were people who knew her name. There were people who wouldn't mind spreading the truth around. One of those people was the man who was currently serving a seven-year sentence for what he did to her. She doubted he would recognise her face—a lot had changed since Dove had been in the man's class—but her name was plastered all over the arrest record.

"Alright, fine. Now go get your hair finished. I need to get this date started. Felicia." Charlie huffed as though it were a great imposition and stalked off, directing his frustrations on a gaffer boy who was holding an apple. Dove let out a breath and closed her eyes.

"Thank you, Wes," she said. "I hadn't even realised that would be an issue."

"Trust me," Wes growled. "When the press get involved, everything is an issue. Now you'd better go do as Wash said. Or we'll both be hung out to dry." He kissed Dove's forehead gently and she felt herself blushing. The other actors were used to their discreet displays of affection—only Roman had made any mention of it, and that had just been a wiggling of his eyebrows that could only be construed as a happy joke —but that didn't stop Dove from blushing.

She ran to do as Wes and Charlie bade and happily let her thoughts settle back on the scene that she was meant to be filming today. The first date between Casey and Vaughn. He was going to be awkward and she was going to be shy. It was so familiar. Dove doubted she would have any issues with her acting today. Or so she hoped; with Charlie, you never knew. Her hair finished and costume fixed, a summery skirt with a light top that was completely inappropriate for the sort of cold weather they had been having recently, Dove walked over to where they were finishing arranging the lighting. Most of the scene would be done through green screen, but even with the backdrops, it was a magical experience to see the set arranged just so.

"You look perfect, Dove, darling," Charlie said. "I mean Felicia."

"That's just for the press," Dove said quietly. Charlie shrugged and moved on while a second assistant placed Dove near a bench and light post. The fake foliage was so realistic that Dove found herself wanting to reach out and touch it. Instead, she did as she was told and sat on the bench, carefully arranging her skirt while she "waited" for Wes-as-Vaughn.

"Casey," Wes said, half-jogging up. He was dressed in dark-blue chinos, a button-up t-shirt and blazer, his hair combed back as the modern styles dictated. It was so unlike him that Dove wanted to laugh. Instead, she pushed her own thoughts aside and did her best to get into character. Casey, on a first date, considering her past issues, would straighten her back and look slightly nervous.

"Hi," she said quietly. Wes leaned in, looking awkward as he did so, and kissed her lightly.

"Hi," he said. Dove touched her fingers to her lips and pulled her brows together. Immediately, Wes was contrite. "Sorry," he apologised profusely. "I... It's just that... this is meant to be a date, not a session, so I thought I would separate the two clearly. Create a boundary."

"It's fine," Dove said. She stood up and smiled slightly. "I, uh, I liked it."

Wes broke out into a grin and nodded eagerly. Dove held out her hand and he took it as though he were being offered a great treasure. Even acting, Dove thought, he knew how to make her feel special. Maybe it was some innate skill that he had, or maybe she was just too used to being invisible, behind the counter of a cafe where all people wanted was a coffee or pastry. She forced her thoughts back into character.

"Where are we going?" she asked. They were meant to have gone to an outdoors arts festival, but with the weather keeping them inside the warehouse, Charlie had conferred with the writers to improvise. And they had come up with having an open-mic event at the bar that featured in the story. Apparently, the writers thought it was a great connecting point in the story and Charlie agreed. Marc had gone out and hired—quietly—a bunch of musicians from a local pub that actually did open-mic nights. They would get little more than twenty pounds and their names in the credits, but most were perfectly willing to do the work.

"It's a surprise," Wes replied. Dove, true to character, shot him a skeptical look and he winced. "Right, you don't like surprises. It's much easier remembering who does and doesn't like what when I have my patient files in front of me."

Dove pressed in closer, entwining her arm with his, forcing them to walk in lockstep. "Well. I'm not a patient at the moment, so there's no hiding behind your folders."

"Now who's the psychiatrist?" Wes teased. He held open the door to the "bar" and Dove stepped inside. Charlie called cut and everything seemed to break into a flurry of action. Before Dove even had time to whisper a comment to Wes, the set had been turned and the bar was in place, the people and musicians set up and a woman with an acoustic guitar on the stage, singing a song that Dove had never heard before. The mic was quiet, so she and Wes could be heard, but the effect was still magical. With a wave of Charlie's hands, everything off set became quiet and the scene picked up exactly where it had left off.

"Oh, wow," Dove said, stepping inside the door. Wes followed and put his hand possessively on the small of her back. She smiled up at him. "This is great."

"Really?" he asked. "Because this is more my age-set and I know that some women don't like going to musical events on a first date because there may be no shared taste in music and—"

"Vaughn," Dove interrupted. "It's great. Really."

"Oh. Okay." Wes shrugged and looked around. "There's a table over there, if you want. I can go grab something to drink."

"Sounds fine." Dove wandered in the direction of the table, fully conscious of the cameras following her. She sat and waited while Wes ordered drinks. Then, Charlie called cut.

"I don't know," he said, walking up to Dove and pouting, one arm supporting the other as he cradled his chin in his hand. "Something just doesn't feel right."

"Should we do the entrance again?" Dove asked. She was beginning to feel the weariness that came with doing a scene over and over and hoped, desperately, that it would just be time for a lunch break.

"I'd love to see that."

Charlie spun around and stared at the newcomer. Dove just furrowed her brow in confusion at the director's shock. Standing at the edge of the line of cameras was a woman dressed in an elegant and obviously quite expensive dress of pastel blue. She had a wrap in a deep green falling off her shoulders and her hair was done up with as much effort as the makeup artists put into Dove's hair. She dangled a bag off her arm and smiled seductively at Charlie. "How are you, Charles?"

Dove turned to Wes to see if he knew who she was, but he was standing at the bar, eyes wide, his skin pale. Charlie walked up to the woman and kissed both of her cheeks. "My goodness, Lise, you haven't changed a bit."

"Thank you, Charles," Lise said, whoever she was. "I heard a rumour from some very good friends of mine in the press that you were doing a new film—a *romance*—and I had to see if those rumours were true. It doesn't look as though I was wrong."

"No." Charlie shook his head. "You weren't wrong."

"So, who's starring?" Lise strolled forwards as though she owned the place and Charlie followed after her, a loyal dog. Even Marc, still shocked, was following at her heels. Dove immediately felt small and drab, though she knew the comparison was ridiculous.

"I am," Wes said. Surprisingly, there was a tone of flat anger in his voice. Dove felt even more confused.

"Well, well, who would have thought?" Lise pulled her eyes up and down Wes' form, a cat eyeing a mouse. "My ex-husband acting in such a lowly romance?"

Now, Dove thought, her heart freezing inside her chest, *Now I feel out of place.*

ell, crap, was Wes' first thought as he saw Lise walking towards him, that all-too-familiar sly smile on her face. He couldn't think any more coherently than that and moving to flee was out of the question. He saw Dove's eyes widening at Lise's words and his initial thought repeated, louder and more emphatically. He was well and truly screwed.

"Weston, darling, how well you look," Lise said, strolling casually across the set as though she owned the place. She reached him and kissed both his cheeks, which he tolerated—barely—and stepped back to examine him. "You've been training, haven't you? I told you that was a good idea."

"Lise," Wes managed. "What are you doing here?"

"I told you," Lise purred, looking around the people gathered on set. She had picked the worst possible day to come barging into things; there were extras strewn all over and there was no doubt that everything that happened was going to end up on the internet. Wes' life was going straight to the dogs and there wasn't a thing he seemed to be able to do to stop it. "I heard from a friend of mine that Charles was doing a film in town and had to stop by. So, who's your counterpart?"

Wes wished fervently that he were dead. Or better yet, very far away. He couldn't seem to speak as Lise dragged her eyes around the female candidates in the room, first discarding the extras then settling on Katie behind the bar. "Are you our starlet? You certainly have the looks for it, but—"

"Actually," Dove stood and faced Lise with the outward expression of complete politeness. Wes' mortification and, yes, fear, rose until his heart was pounding in his head. "I'm acting as counterpart to Wes."

Lise turned, every perfectly sculpted—and surgically maintained—piece of her radiating shock. It was the closest anyone had got to talking back to her in a long time, Wes imagined. But Dove just stood there, a pleasant smile on her face that didn't quite reach her eyes. Her smiles almost never reached her eyes, lessening the sad depths, but Wes had grown more accustomed to her full smile. Now, he just felt badly, as though he should have prepared her for Lise. Not that Wes had ever expected to see her again. Especially considering what Wash had done for him to sort things out. That was the whole reason he was here, after all.

"You certainly are unique." Lise strode towards Dove with every critical bone in her body on full display. She held out her hand and Dove took it. The connection was dropped a moment later. "I'm Lise Blackwood," she said, her eyes flicking to Wes seductively.

"Felicia Teague," Dove lied effortlessly, her skill at acting making certain that no hint of any hesitation showed. Wes would have given just about anything to know what she was really thinking. He wanted to take her aside and ask, tucking that ever-present strand of hair behind her ear and making certain that she knew everything was going to be alright. Instead he was forced to watch as his world fell apart. At least, it felt that way.

"So, what's it like acting across my ex-husband? He can be a bit intense, you know. When he sets his mind on something, he won't stop until it's conquered." Lise shrugged one shoulder and raised her eyebrows, expecting Dove to react. Dove merely nodded.

"It shows in the quality of his work," she said. "I hate to be rude, but we really must get back to work. Charlie only has the musicians for today."

Lise blinked, taken aback. Wes knew she was trying to goad Dove into asking questions and prying about her relationship with Wes. He also knew that if Lise had her way, she would be spreading lies about the two of them from here to France. So by denying her the chance to begin her manipulations, Dove effectively shut her down. It was, frankly, fascinating to watch.

She nodded and smiled. "Of course! Here I am, interrupting. I'll just stand over with Marc and watch, if that's alright?" Her tone of voice brooked no argument and she was already walking over to the wide-eyed assistant when Wes found his words.

"No," he growled, his voice carrying as though he were on a stage rather than a film set. It was loud enough to make Wash raise his eyebrows in surprise and Marc recoil. Dove did nothing but tug at the fabric of her dress, as though it were crooked. Wes recognised it as one of her nervous tics and wished that he could have avoided all of this.

"I beg your pardon?" Lise asked, turning and facing Wes with one hip cocked. That move had been known to drive Wes either to his knees or the punching bag in his flat. This time, he was not going to let it affect him.

"No. It's not alright if you stay and watch," Wes growled. He knew that all of the people there were eagerly getting the show they had hoped for and was even more infuriated by that fact. There was no other way to deal with Lise, though, than a public denial. And this was about as public as it could get. "You don't belong here. I don't care who you think your friends are, but you have no right to be here and you need to leave."

"What right do you have to tell me to leave?" Lise huffed. "If you recall, we're not married anymore."

"Exactly," Wes snapped, his voice sharp. "You were allowed certain privileges while we were married. Now? You're just getting in the way."

"Wes," Wash warned, his voice quiet. Lise grabbed onto that like a lifeline.

"You're not in charge here, Weston." Lise sidled up to Wash and threaded her arm through his. He shrugged her out of his grip, but she was unperturbed. "If Charles wants me to go, then I will, but *you* have no authority over me." That last phrase sounded like a challenge, one that Wes would have gladly met three years ago. Now, he just wanted her gone so he could go to Dove and explain everything, wrapping her in his arms and making certain she knew that his past was just that. Past.

"You should go, Lise," Wash said flatly. She recoiled as if stung and stared at Wash with all the shock her meagre acting skills possessed. "And please don't come back. You're more trouble than you're worth. Which is exactly why, if you recall, that I was a witness for Wes in your divorce."

"Bastard," Lise whispered, tears springing to her eyes. Wes doubted they were real, but the effect was similar. She hadn't cared about Wash's allegiance when she strolled into the warehouse a few minutes ago. Was it only a few minutes? It felt an eternity and everything had seemed to go downhill from there. Lise raised her hand as if to slap Wash, who stood perfectly still and calm, saying nothing, then she turned and ran from the building as quickly as her spike heels would allow.

Wes waited until the door had slammed behind her before letting his shoulders slump. Wash squeezed the bridge of his nose in frustration. Marc came up behind the director and the two exchanged words for a few moments. Wes focused his attention on Dove, who was focusing her attention on Wash. It wasn't done to be cruel, of that Wes was certain, but it stung nonetheless.

"Okay!" Wash clapped his hands together, gathering the full attention of everyone in the room. "We're going to take our lunch break now. You have two hours, but if you're late, you'll be staying overtime. And if I hear even a whisper of what just happened on any internet page or social media forum, news stream or anything, I'll file suit against every single one of you." With that, he turned and stalked off towards his office, Marc hurrying behind him.

The extras looked at one another, worried whispers starting up almost immediately. They quickly filed out of the warehouse as if glad to be free of that place. The techies followed, as did Roman and Katie and the other actors. Finally, only Wes was left with Dove. He walked up behind her and put a hand on her shoulder. To her credit, she didn't flinch, though he could feel her tense.

"Would you like to get some lunch?" Wes asked. Dove said nothing. He sat in one of the chairs across from her and looked at her. She looked as she ever did, quietly beautiful with deep blue eyes that held immeasurable sadness. She bit her bottom lip and took in a breath.

"Are you alright?" she said finally. Wes blinked. That was the last thing he had expected her to say.

Given that it was Dove, though, he shouldn't have been surprised. She would think of him before herself. Still.

"Am I alright? You've just had my entire messy past thrown in your face and you're asking if I'm alright?" Wes said, trying not to sound too incredulous. Amazed, he thought. Go for amazed.

Dove replied with a weak smile. She took another deep breath and focused her gaze on her hands, which were sitting perfectly still on the table. "I'm trying really hard not to be selfish," she said.

"What? You're not selfish, Dove."

"Then why do I want to snap at you for keeping this from me? She walked in here and said who she was and my first thought wasn't surprise or shock or anything like that," Dove breathed. Her tone made Wes suddenly want to block his ears. He didn't want to hear this. But he had to. It was his own fault for causing her hurt. "It was that she was..." Dove lifted her eyes to look at him. "She was me, before I came. I was afraid that I would be discarded like that and become hurt and lonely and cynical."

"Cynical, yes, but Lise is anything from hurt and lonely," Wes retorted quietly. Dove shook her head.

"That look in her eyes when she saw you? When she realised that I was acting with you? That was pain. Hidden by arrogance and seduction, but it was still pain," Dove murmured. "I didn't want to be like that."

"Dove, I would neve—"

"Then I looked at you," she interrupted, "and I wondered how I could be so selfish. You were hurt, worse than she was, and you were terrified and embarrassed. There's obviously a lot of history there that I don't understand. What I do understand is having a pain in your past rear up its head to bite you in the ass. Yours isn't as visible as mine, perhaps, but it's there. Which is why I'm asking, Wes, are you alright?"

Wes wanted to throw his hands up and roar in frustration. Dove was probably the most selfless person he knew. She put everyone else before herself, giving up so much without ever asking for anything in return. Just look at Meg and Timmy, sharing her flat and getting paid. Okay, so Meg was managing the cafe, but that was also a gift. Then there was her working for Wash, probably for comparably little, because he needed her. Or thought he did. Now she was sitting there, freely admitting that she was having a hard time with Wes' ex-wife showing up out of the blue and she was saying that didn't matter. It was amazing, but also frustrating.

"I've had worse," was what Wes said instead. He shook his head. "How about we go to lunch and I'll tell you the whole story?"

"I don't imagine it's a long story," Dove said with a wry smile. "You fell for her charm, she happily took you in, things were good and then they weren't. Charlie helped you out and that's how you ended up here, on the set of a romantic drama."

"It's slightly more complicated than that," Wes said, "but that's most of it. Am I that transparent?"

Dove shook her head. "Not you, but her. She needs

the world to bend to her whims and expects that it will. When it doesn't, things go badly. Many people have a desperate need to control their world. It comes from dealing with the unknown purpose of the universe."

"I keep forgetting you read philosophy," Wes chuckled. "You have a knack for figuring people out."

"It's... a learned skill," Dove flicked her eyes to the table. "Comes from seeking out threats."

And there he was feeling terrible again. Of course it would have been a defence mechanism derived from her experience, not learned from books. Wes wondered if it would be possible to just go home for the rest of the day and hope that everything would be forgotten tomorrow. "Sorry," he murmured. "I didn't mean... come on. Let's go get something to eat."

"You seem to have a fixation on lunch." Dove's half-smile was back, which Wes took to be a good sign. She pushed back from the table and stood. "Come on, you can buy me tea and biscuits and tell me about your past love, just in case I need to defend myself again."

Wes nodded and the two walked to a nearby cafe where they could sit in a corner in peace. He knew that after the press conference tomorrow, the chance of them getting out without being spotted and assaulted by interested parties was going to drop considerably, so he determined to make the best of the opportunity while he could. Dove seemed to be ignorant of what would happen and went about ordering tea and a pastry with her usual regularity.

Wes didn't realise until they were seated at the

table and the tea was before him that he wanted to talk about Lise. He wanted to tell Dove what went on between them and have her understand that what he had now was completely different. It would do to soothe her worries and his own and, like her own past, it was something he didn't talk about. He wanted to share that with her.

"We met when I was... probably about your age," Wes started. He laughed drily. "It makes me feel old to say such things."

"You're only as old as you believe you are," Dove replied. "If it helps, the universe is billions upon billions of years older than you are. You're just a speck of dust in comparison to the universe, not old at all."

"That doesn't help, but thank you anyways. No, I was still fairly new to things, but my agents were talking quietly for a deal that would make my career. I was about to be big and then Lise appeared. She was young—barely an adult—but just as cunning as she is now. She knew her way around and had connections with talent scouts, agents, reporters. She knew that I was going to do well and started hanging around set. It was gratifying and a huge ego boost to have a beautiful woman following me around. I didn't even care that she got involved with my agents in order to further my career. It was as you said: she called and I came.

"It was like that for years, her pushing my career along without my input, or in most cases, knowledge of what was going on. Then, by the point I figured it out, I was already famous enough that I didn't need to skate by taking whatever role I could get. I had the choicest options handed to me on a silver platter, relatively speaking. I had more money than I knew what to do with. People wanted to know my opinion on things that I had no right to give advice on. Lise, for all her planning and manipulating, had failed to account for the fact that my career excelled and hers did not. Sure, she had connections almost everywhere, but very few of them were actually willing to give her an acting job. She just wasn't that good. I was. It became a huge point of contention between us.

"She claimed she sacrificed everything for me, I pointed out that I had never asked for her help to begin with. The arguments got out of hand very quickly. It was to the point that I had to buy a flat—my current one—and abandon our house because I couldn't live there with her. She took to holding extravagant parties, imbibing in alcohol, marijuana and who knows what else. When I walked in on her with another man, though, that was it for me. I can handle a lot, but adultery is the most complete act of betrayal to me. So I filed for divorce, had Wash witness for me—in exchange for a favour—and we went our separate ways. Unfortunately for Lise, the fact that I was the one getting the work meant that those connections who had been willing to help her help me gave up on her and backed me. I never wanted it. It just..."

Wes trailed off, his words gone. He had nothing more that he could say to explain what had happened. He could go into details about how violent Lise got when she was drunk or high or both, how much of his money she squirrelled away, what she did to try and blackball his name in the industry, how she slandered his name to reporters, but none of that mattered. It was only a part of the whole, a problem that had been so deep-rooted that it had taken two years of arguing to sort out. Even then, Wes still felt a sore spot near his sternum when he thought about how the woman he had once loved had betrayed him. The image of Lise with her lover was forever burned into his mind, the picture coming forth during bouts of anger or when—

Dove put her hand on his and squeezed his fingers lightly. He lifted his gaze from his tea to her eyes and saw sympathy for his pain there, as well as understanding. "Those things which we do not ask for are often the ones with the deepest impacts," she said softly. Wes nodded and tried to smile, managing only a slight twitch of his mouth.

"I didn't ask for you," he breathed and Dove nodded.

"Nor I you," she said, squeezing his fingers again.

18

"We're here today with renowned director Charles Wash to talk about his latest film, *Closing the Distance*. Charlie, you've done a number of big-hit action, thriller, and drama films. What made you decide to do a romance?" The reporter was a good-looking young woman with the looks of someone plucked right out of university specifically for her looks. She was leaning slightly forwards to show her interest in Charlie, her gaze intense.

"Well, you're right. With my past films, romance is something that I've generally stayed away from. There are a dozen romance movies for every good thriller or drama. But they also have the reputation of being fake, unrealistic, even cliché. I want to change that. Romance itself is one of the most profound things a person can experience. So why, in an industry that can change the way people look at the world, is love something to be scoffed at? With this film, I'm going to change perspectives and give people something real." Charlie nodded and looked at the reporter, completely ignoring the cameras. He might have been more frequently behind the cameras, but he certainly had presence before them as well.

Dove hoped that she would be able to express a similar sort of confidence. The reporter was enthralled with Charlie and kept asking him questions, such as how he hoped to show his artistic vision and why he had decided to pursue a dramatic piece and more. Then she started asking questions about casting and Dove felt her belly clench. She would be up soon.

Wes, thankfully, was called up first, being the big name in the industry. He, too, had an easy rapport with the reporter, though Dove imagined the woman was mostly just in awe of Wes. They discussed his prolific career and the fact that he hadn't dabbled in romance movies since he was quite a bit younger. "Why now? Because Wash needed a favour and I owed him one."

"Care to elaborate on that?" The woman leaned in more, her shirt and jacked hugging her curves in a fairly blatant attempt to capture Wes' interest. He ignored such manoeuvres and merely shook his head.

"There's nothing to elaborate," he said. "I owed him a favour. Besides, it's been fun. There's not as much drama as on some of the other sets I've had. The cast and crew are all very professional."

"That's interesting." The reporter nodded. "I hear that almost half of the main cast are new to the film industry, including your romantic interest. Can you introduce us to her?"

Wes nodded and Dove felt like flinching away, or perhaps running and hiding. She disliked this sort of thing. A lot. "Sure. This is Felicia Teague." He held out his hand towards Dove and she rose from her seat, moving towards him and into the light and camera frame. She knew the session was being recorded and not live, and that she had been in front of cameras for the last few months without issue, but somehow, this was different. This was real, not her portraying a character. Then she considered the fact that she was using an assumed name and realised she *was* portraying a character. The thought didn't help, no matter how much she wanted it to.

"Felicia!" The reporter smiled brightly at Dove and looked her over. "You look lovely. Not at all what I expected, but from what Charlie and Weston have described, you fit the part perfectly. I think it's your eyes."

Dove inclined her head. "Thank you," she said. She hoped that she was smiling.

"So, what was it like being introduced to the film industry and realising that you would be acting across Weston here? Quite a shock, I'm sure," the woman said. She looked eagerly at Dove as though hoping for some juicy gossip and Dove flashed a desperate expression to Wes. They had agreed to keep their relationship quiet, and she wasn't sure what to say. Actually, her lack of locution had nothing to do with their relationship, just fear pressing down on her chest. She felt the familiar bile of panic in her throat; the situation was too much like the trial of the man who raped her for her liking.

"Actually, Felicia had no idea who I was," Wes interceded, shaking his head in mock disappointment. "She was more concerned with picking out a sandwich to be concerned with me."

"Is that true?" The reporter turned to Dove to confirm the statement and Dove bit her lip, nodding and trying not to blush.

"I don't watch many movies," Dove said by way of explanation. The reporter laughed and Dove found herself chuckling along with the woman. Some of the tension in her chest released and she found herself more able to answer the questions.

The interview lasted for about half-an-hour, with questions being aimed at what Dove thought of the industry, what it was like to be on camera for the first time, what she thought of her character and the story and what it was like working with Charlie and Wes. As the interview progressed, she found it easier to talk, giving up a few anecdotes while keeping the more personal pieces to herself. She didn't even feel as though the reporter was trying to trip her up, just getting her to converse naturally. Of course, this conversation was one that would end up all over the world thanks to the internet, but still, it was far more casual than she had thought. The reporter was thrilled and finally released Dove and Wes in order to talk with the rest of the cast and some of the crew, including Marc.

Dove waited until she was in her dressing room with Wes and the door was closed safely behind them before she let out a shaky laugh and sank onto the couch in relief. "It wasn't that bad," Wes pointed out. Dove shook her head. "You're lucky you're just starting out. They go easy on you for that. And they went easy on me for that, too, so thanks."

"It wasn't that bad," Dove agreed, "but that doesn't mean I ever want to do something like that again. That was worse than any job interview I've ever had. What was it like changing costumes in front of people? I mean, really!"

"Surely it wasn't the worst thing you've ever done," Wes sat on the couch beside Dove and she leaned into him, relaxing further as his arm wrapped around her shoulder.

"No," Dove murmured. "The trial was far worse."

Wes tensed and cursed quietly. "I'm sorry. I didn't mean to bring up bad memories."

"It's fine," Dove said. "That was when I got to watch him be sentenced. I was free—injured, but free—and he wasn't. Things only got better from there."

"And now you're here with an old man, having just been roped into giving an interview," Wes joked. Dove lidded her eyes and turned her face up to his.

"Hardly old," she said. "You keep up with me just fine."

"I suppose," Wes drew out the last word and Dove chuckled.

She pushed herself up so that she could kiss him and he grinned under her lips. The feeling, for some reason, of his skin against hers and their mouths touching, moving together, felt more electrical and charged than it had before. Dove felt her skin shiver with the charge and knew, without a doubt, that she had fallen in love with Wes. He was the only person she had told her secrets to and he trusted her enough in return to tell her of his own past. He could comfort her with a simple look and she knew immediately when he came into a room. Her own logic told her that it was far more than lust. What she felt then, wanting to devour him with her mouth? That was lust. This feeling that was crushing her chest so she couldn't breathe unless he was there? That was love. Now if she could just figure out some way to show him.

Dove deepened the kiss before swinging her legs over his to straddle his lap. Wes made a surprised noise in his throat and pulled back, staring at her in surprise. "Dove?" he asked, his voice low with need. She could feel his desire in the pounding of his blood and the tightness of his trousers between her. This was not a time for words, though. So she just smiled and brushed her hand across his cheek. He smiled. Then, she twitched her hips, grinding into him.

"Dove!" Wes gasped, his hands moving almost instinctively to her hips, his fingers digging into her skin. It wasn't a sign for her to stop, though, Dove knew. It was the way that he helped guide her hips, moving when she moved. She leaned down and kissed his jaw, pressing her chest into his. Wes let out a sigh and lay his forehead against her chest, breathing hard. "Dove," he said, his voice little more than a whisper. "Don't."

"Why not?" Dove asked, leaning back just enough to give them some air. "I want this. I know exactly what I'm doing. There's no panic, no fear."

"I believe you," Wes murmured. He captured her mouth for a light kiss. "And I trust you. But don't do this, not right now."

Dove pulled back farther, nursing a touch of hurt in her chest. "You don't want this?" she breathed, unsure how she could have misread everything so completely. Wes tightened his grip on her waist, bringing her close for a hug.

"You have no idea how much I want this," he said. Dove smiled. She kissed his neck. "But I also don't want this to happen between us here. In your dressing room. After having been shredded by reporters. I may be old fashioned, but I want it to be special. To mean something."

Dove's smile widened and she pressed her nose into the crook of Wes' neck, breathing in his scent, feeling his pulse throb beneath his skin. "You old romantic," she murmured. "I never would have guessed."

"What, the wine and chocolate the first week didn't give it away?" Wes chuckled, the sound rumbling against Dove's ear. He wrapped his arms around her waist. "Tell me you understand. Tell me that you're not upset."

"How could I be upset?" Dove asked. She shifted so that she was sitting next to him, her head leaning against his shoulder. "You're the first person to ever care that much. To act like it means something to do it right. To consider me as a person, not as…"

Wes brushed his fingers beneath her chin, nudging her to look up at him. "Hey. Listen to me. You are worth something. You are valuable. And don't you ever let anyone tell you differently, okay?"

Dove could think of several snarky things to say, to chide him that he had thought she didn't value herself. To tease him. To make him laugh, and lighten the mood. Instead, she just rested her head on his shoulder. "Thank you, Wes," she murmured.

They lay there on the couch for an indeterminate amount of time. Dove didn't want to move, her body melted from her exertions with the reporters and that bone-deep happiness that came from love. Wes' fingers danced in patterns on her skin and neither spoke. Dove was afraid that she would break the spell that seemed to surround them. Wes, on the other hand, seemed pensive. It didn't matter. The quiet brush of his fingers on her bare arm and the complete satisfaction she felt with life at the moment led Dove to sigh deeply and close her eyes. She fell into a quiet doze, her thoughts floating with the sensations she had awakened that she had never known before.

Even the knocking on the door couldn't bother Dove. She heard Wes curse and he moved away from her to answer the door, grabbing a blanket on the way and draping it over her shoulders. She just continued to doze, moments away from sleep. She heard Wes answer and Charlie's voice talking to him. The words were nothing but garble in her half-dazed state. At Charlie's shocked whistle, though, she roused her mind enough to listen to what was happening.

"Wes, you look as though you've just had quite the adventure," Charlie said, his voice quiet and sounding perilously like a snicker. Wes growled, but didn't respond to the jibe. Dove found herself pleased with that and moved back to sleep. Then Charlie spoke again. "I didn't think that you would seduce her so quickly, or so thoroughly, but then it has been a few months, hasn't it? Oh, don't protest, your hair and that spot on your neck tells me everything. When you repay a favour, you do it thoroughly, don't you?"

Dove was immediately awake, her body frozen in place at the words. *Repay a favour. Seduce her.* She realised exactly what had been happening and cursed herself for being so stupid that she hadn't realised it before. Wes, older, wiser, handsome enough that he could have any woman he wanted, and successful enough to keep her, was only on the set of the movie because he was repaying a favour. Dove, apparently, was part of that repayment. And why not? It would serve to make her relax, make her acting more realistic. And when the time came for the more intimate scenes of the film, then she wouldn't be too nervous, because it was with him. All of that was plainly before her.

No wonder he hadn't wanted to have sex with her. She was glad for that, at least, because she wasn't certain that the shame that rose up and broke over her heart would have let her keep on going if she had managed to accomplish her goal. The only problem was, that bone-crushing feeling of love that had urged her to give herself to Wes was still there. And it was causing her more pain than any pleasure she had ever known. To love someone who didn't love you in return and worse, was only using you, was close to lethal. How could she have been so naïve? Especially after all she'd been through, especially once she'd understood that the world was out for itself.

Dove sucked in a breath, seeing black spots before her eyes. The spots cleared, but when she sat up, she saw Wes leaning against the now-closed door. His hair was dishevelled from where Dove had run her fingers through it, and there was indeed a red spot forming where she'd worried at his neck. She wasn't surprised Charlie had formed the conclusion he had. She resisted the urge to glare daggers at Wes. He stared at Dove, wide-eyed.

"I thought you were asleep," he said, sounding stricken. And why shouldn't he? A flash of anger ran through Dove and she curled her lip at him, feeling disgusted with herself.

"Get out," she said, her voice flat. Wes opened his

mouth to say something, but Dove wanted none of that. "Get out."

He did, gathering his phone and slipping out the door like a ghost. One that was going to haunt her for as long as she lived.

19

The worse part was her eyes. Wes would find himself looking into them on set—practically the only time Dove interacted with him—and see her pain reflected there. She had always had sad eyes, but now the sadness was his fault. It was excruciating.

After Wash had ruined everything, even if it was an accident, Wes had staggered into his dressing room and tried to think of something to do to salvage the situation. Not that he blamed Wash. The director had meant well, and he didn't know that Wes was already in love with Dove. Wes had thought her asleep, otherwise he would have shoed Wash far away and gone to be with her. He couldn't even explain to the director that they hadn't had sex, that it wasn't like that because then he would have to explain *why*, and he wouldn't do that to Dove. No, it was his own fault, for not being sensitive enough to realise she was awake, for not being brave enough to tell her his feelings before, for being a coward.

And he was still a coward. A week after the incident and Wes still hadn't managed to explain to Dove what the truth was. She avoided him, true, but he also didn't go seek her out. It was too painful to see what destruction he had wrought. So he tortured himself by playing the happy-in-love Vaughn on camera, who was interacting with the beautiful-in-love Casey. She was beautiful, too. Every day, she seemed to grow more beautiful to him. Her soft features, the grace with which she moved, the smiles tossed so casually as she played Casey that vanished as soon as the cameras were off. The pain grew worse as he realised the distance between them was growing.

No one else knew. No one could tell that Dove no longer wanted anything to do with him. Wash kept giving Wes knowing glances and everyone else was acting normally. They talked, they laughed, they didn't seem affected at all when the earth shattered beneath Wes' feet. Everyone except Dove. It was torture.

Instead of going out with her at nights, trying to find places where people wouldn't bother them, Wes simply went back to his flat. The first few nights, he had been so angry he pounded into his punching bag for an hour. As time moved on, though, he was nothing but weary. The only thing that kept him going was the fact that he would see Dove the next day. It was a foolish hope, but he kept thinking that maybe he would get the chance to sit down and explain things and that she would forgive him, just as she had regarding Lise, but each day passed with no communication between them. Their characters talked and Wes found himself living for those moments, pretending that it was Dove saying those things, not Casey. Pretending that he was Vaughn, not an idiot who had messed everything up.

Then, a week after the incident, as Wes liked to call it in his mind, Wash approached him. "We're going to do the intimate scenes tomorrow."

Wes nearly choked on his coffee. "What?"

"I want to do it before the honeymoon period between you two wears off. Not to mention that we've got a good deal of filming done. There aren't all that many scenes left between you two, so I want to get everything finished. Then we can work on the scenes between you and Roman or Dove and Rachel. It makes sense," Wash said. Marc nodded fervently behind him and Wes looked into his coffee. The taste was too bitter and the whisky didn't help. He couldn't very well tell Wash that things had gone sideways, either, because it would cause a whole lot of problems that he didn't have the heart to deal with.

"Alright," Wes said. What else could he say? He hid his trepidation with a swift drink of the coffee. The alcohol burned slightly going down, but it was a welcome pain. He wouldn't drink enough to lose his inhibitions. It was enough to take the edge off, and that was all that mattered.

"Great. Have you seen Dove this morning?" Wash looked around.

"She probably stopped by the cafe," Wes said, hoping his lack of knowledge about her whereabouts didn't give him away. Wash nodded.

"I told her she didn't have to be in until ten today, but I thought she might be in slightly earlier. Then, you're working, so she wouldn't get to talk with you." Wash shrugged and waved his hand dismissively. "Go to makeup and get kitted out, okay? I have to have words with our newest cameraman about the meaning of 'steady cam'."

"Right. Okay." Wes started turning towards the makeup department when Wash put a hand on his arm.

"Hey, are you alright? You seem a little out of it. Is this about the press junket? I promise it was all good. I made sure of it, in fact." Wash frowned. He rarely held such a serious expression. The concern made Wes want to shout and accuse Wash of ruining everything he had with Dove, but shame held him back.

Wes lifted his coffee and shrugged. "Coffee hasn't started working yet. That's all."

"If you're sure," Wash said in that caring tone that reminded Wes why they were friends. Good ones. Wes nodded and the director let go of his arm, letting Wes flee the scene and escape into makeup. It was far easier to pretend to be someone else at this point than it was to be himself. So he let Wes Blackwood fade away and Vaughn come out. For the remainder of the day, that was all there was. Vaughn whose only goal was to help Casey because he was desperately in love.

Dove did the same, pretending only to be Casey. Wes knew because she smiled as she always had and Wash rarely had to have her stop and fix something. They managed to film straight through almost two whole scenes that day, getting multiple takes and different angles. Dove and Wes worked together as they always had and no one could tell the difference between today and any other day. As far as anyone could tell, everything was perfect.

That is, until Dove approached Wes at the end of the day. She looked weary—bone weary, not just tired from being on her feet all day—and had both hands clutching the shoulder strap of her satchel as if it were the only thing grounding her to this reality.

Wes opened his mouth to speak, "Dove, I—"

"Please don't," she said. Her voice sounded as it always had: calm and collected. Underneath that, there was a note of disappointment that Wes knew was his fault. "I don't need to hear your explanations. I know why you did it. I understand. I don't approve of what you did, but I understand."

"Dove," Wes started again, this time unable to hide the anguish in his own tone. His acting for the day was, apparently, done.

"No," she said, voice perilously close to snapping. Dove sighed and shifted her weight. "Look, I just wanted to tell you that Charlie says we're doing the... intimate scenes tomorrow. I don't expect it to be, well, like it was—almost was—but know that I'll be okay. You don't need to... Please don't say anything or get involved if there are issues."

"After what I did, you just expect to be able to go on camera and film that without an issue? I mean, I know it's not real sex, but after what happened to you—"

This time, Dove didn't cut him off by speaking. She just flicked her eyes to his and Wes saw the overwhelming anger there. Sadness was still present and almost impossible to ignore, but more than that was her anger. It was fiery and wrathful and growing. Wes nodded and said nothing, bowing his head in acquiescence. Dove jerked her head firmly and they walked out of the building together, for all appearances the same camaraderie between them that there had always been.

That night, Wes slept hardly at all. He woke twice from night sweats and once from the mistaken idea that Dove was calling him. At nearly four thirty in the morning, he gave up on sleep altogether and just sat on his bed, staring out the window as the dawn began and the day turned into a grey day full of drizzle. He held his phone in his hand, the overwhelming urge to call someone—*anyone*—and tell them everything. The only problem was that the person he really wanted to call wanted absolutely nothing to do with him. The others wouldn't understand.

Wes sighed and went to take a shower, throwing his phone on his bed in disgust. He spent far too long under the hot spray of the water and by the time he was done, the water had gone cold and he was shivering. It definitely wasn't a great start to the day. He then wandered into the kitchen and saw the paper from his personal trainer for his diet taped to the fridge. In a snarl of pure anger, Wes ripped the paper from the fridge and tore it into several pieces. He felt slightly better and decided that perhaps he should exercise a bit.

An hour later, Wes was still pounding away at his heavy bag, his muscles protesting and his lips curled back in a snarl. Sweat dripped into his eyes and he knew he was going to need another shower. But he couldn't seem to stop. All his frustrations were focused in each hit on the bag and if he stopped now then they would just build up again. So he kept going, far beyond the point when he should have called it quits. Eventually, his body just gave out on him and Wes couldn't keep his hands up any longer. His legs trembled and he had to sit or they would have collapsed, too. More sweat fell down his face and Wes wiped it away. He realised, then, that it wasn't sweat but his own tears.

"Damn it," he said, voice choked. He hated being this weak. But he couldn't fix this. Not with the way things stood.

"What happened?" Wash asked. Wes looked up, somehow not surprised that the director was in his flat. He had given the small, vibrant man a key years ago, in the midst of the issues with Lise. Even then, Wes didn't think that things had been this bad. At least, he hadn't felt this anguish in his chest. Anger, sure, disappointment, absolutely, but not anguish. Not absolute pain at the thought of losing her.

"You did," Wes said with a breathy laugh that held no humour.

"Did I?" Wash replied, sitting on the ground next to Wes. "If I thought you hated her so much, I wouldn't have—"

"Hate her?" Wes interrupted. "I don't hate her. I don't think it's possible to hate her."

"Then what? You've been like this for a while, now," Wash said. Wes took a deep breath and pushed his damp hair from his eyes. He carefully peeled the MMA gloves from his hands and threw them across the flat. With all of the strength he had just used beating the crap out of a helpless bag, the gloves went about a metre. Wash arched his eyebrow at Wes.

"That day you came in and found us... when you thought we'd had sex, which we hadn't—" Wes started. He rubbed his eyes and shook his head. "She heard you."

"I see," Wash said, his voice far too calm for what Wes was feeling. He wanted to shout at the man and demand to know what he was thinking, but he was too weak. So Wes shrugged with one shoulder.

"Do you?" he asked quietly. "I may have started out 'seducing' her on your orders, but things... changed."

"Ah," Wash replied, his lips drawing into a thoughtful line. "You fell in love with the girl. And she with you, obviously, or you wouldn't have... well, *not* slept with her. Or was she just interested in you for your fame? I wouldn't have thought she would be interested in such things, but I admit I hired her rather quickly."

Wes said nothing. Wash was right and that made things all the more painful. To do something like Dove had done—to admit her trust in him, to initiate such intimate contact, even if it ultimately hadn't gone anywhere—meant that she had to have been in love with him. After what she had experienced, what else could it have been? Lust? He scoffed at such a notion.

So she was in love with him and then heard what Wash said. Wes felt even more the villain. He turned his head to look at Wash, who, to his credit, was looking slightly guilty at his part in things. Wes hung his head and stared at the ground, knowing that he had to explain everything or it would be pointless. "Did you know she had been raped?"

Wash sucked in a sharp breath. For a moment, Wes felt even more guilty. He knew it had to be done, though. Wash was one of his only true friends and he had to understand what Dove was going through. Had to understand how much pain she was experiencing. That it wasn't Wes who needed the comfort, but her.

Wash shuddered. "I thought she had been bullied or maybe tightly controlled by her father. Her relationship with her brother was only more proof of that. But *that*? I didn't know."

Wes said nothing. He had run out of words to say. Nothing could explain what he was feeling and what he felt he had lost.

"She loved you. And you... you did fall in love with her, didn't you?" Wash asked. Wes nodded, defeated. "Then I made the foolish mistake of speaking out of turn. Now she won't speak to you outside of filming? I see."

Wes nodded. "It's as though I betrayed her. And I can't get her to listen to me. I can't explain."

Wash said nothing for a moment. Each second that passed was a nail in the coffin for Wes; if Wash didn't know how to fix this, then he was doomed. "I knew how to help you when Lise was causing problems. Help you divorce her, get her out of your life. This is entirely different. I cannot force her to listen to you."

"All I need is the chance," Wes said. For a brief instant, hope flared through him and he felt as though he could move again.

"I'll do my best," Wash offered. "For now, though, I came to fetch you to the warehouse. You missed call time."

That explained things, Wes thought. He put his hands on either side of him and pushed off the ground, using every ounce of spare energy he had. His hope of reconnecting with Dove was all that was getting him through. Wash forced a protein shake into his hand and Wes drank it as though it were a lifeline. In a way, it was. He would never make it through today if he didn't have some extra help.

They arrived at the warehouse within the hour, Wes still sweaty from his workout and Wash looking grim. The first thing Wes noted was the fact that there was hardly anyone there. Most of the tech crew was missing and there were only a few people on cameras, doubling as lighting and sound crew. The only actor there was Dove and even Marc was nowhere to be seen, though Wes imagined the assistant was holed away in an office doing paperwork.

Wash walked up to Dove and Wes trailed behind. She was stunning, Wes thought, even looking slightly nervous. She wore a dress that he had seen her in before as part of filming. Her hair and makeup were done, though there was no one around to do it. Wes' heart fluttered at the sight of her and yet she tensed up when she saw him.

"Dove, darling, you look lovely." Wash went up to her and hugged her. An irrational surge of jealousy hit Wes, but he managed to push it down.

"Where is everybody?" Dove asked quietly, returning the hug with half the enthusiasm the director showed. Wash shot Wes a look and frowned.

"They took the day off. I didn't want a bunch of people standing around, staring. This isn't a pornography. This is tasteful and dramatic. Besides, we can manage on our own, can't we?" Wash asked. Dove nodded and bit her lip, flicking her eyes to Wes for a bare fraction of a second. That second was enough to make the kernel of hope flare. She didn't say anything, only nodded again. Wes shifted his weight and tried to silently signal Wash, to see if the director would say anything. The man only gave Wes a significant look and pointedly looked at the stairs to the dressing rooms. Wes understood, but that didn't mean he liked it. Wash wanted to have a word with Dove alone.

Wes went up the stairs and to his dressing room, washing up and preparing his costume and makeup swiftly. Having been in the film industry for so long, he was capable enough at such things. As there was no one else on set that day, it was necessary. He knew that, but every instinct he had told him that he should be on the stairs, listening to the conversation Wash and Dove were having. It could decide his future, for one thing. With that thought in mind, Wes finished preparing as quickly as possible and dashed out to the stairs. He stayed up as far as he could while still being able to hear—it would only make everything worse to get caught eavesdropping.

"...It's not that I was trying to be cruel," Wash said, sounding distressed. "I was just trying to make things easier on you. If you were more comfortable, then things would be better for you."

"And for you," Dove replied. Her voice was soft, hardly accusing, but Wes imagined that the barb was felt all the same. After all, he felt it, so Wash, whose idea it had been to begin with, would feel it more. "I'm not blaming you for wanting a smooth filming. Everyone wants things to go well."

"But..." Wash prompted. Dove was silent for a moment. Wes could almost visualise her tugging at her dress or sitting down in one of the chairs.

"I would have liked to have been given the chance on my own," Dove murmured. "I'm sorry," she apologised almost immediately, probably in some reaction to Wash's expression. "This isn't one of those things you can outline in a contract. And you *were* trying to make things easier on everyone."

"Dove. Darling," Wash said, soothing and somehow far calmer than Wes would have been in that situation. "I am sorry for not having faith in you. I wasn't quite sure what to expect; you'd never done this before, not even in making videos for the internet, and I wanted you to feel this was where you belonged. My motives weren't entirely altruistic, but I was thinking of you."

"I know," Dove said. Quiet acceptance of his apology. Should Wes move, now? Go apologise for his own part in things? Something told him to stay exactly where he was.

"You really should hear Wes out, you know," Wash said. There was a pause, too long for a conventional conversation and Wes filled it with the pounding of his heart in his ears. He clenched his fist at his side, knuckles turning white. "He was acting on my behalf. He didn't want to deceive you."

"Then why?" Dove asked, her voice almost a cry. Wes rose and went down the stairs, unable to stand back and listen any longer. Dove turned to face him, her eyes wary and accusing. She had been crying, her mascara running, her arms wrapped around her waist. The makeup would have to be redone, but to Wes she had never been more beautiful. Vulnerable and a little angry, she was hurting. She was flawed.

But she was human and he was desperately in love with her.

"Because I owed Wash for saving me from a life with Lise. But you have to believe me, Dove, as soon as we sat down and had a real conversation, I wasn't just acting. I really did like you. I really did—do. I really do think you're the most beautiful creature I've ever seen. I've never told anyone but Wash about all the things Lise did and I've never felt less deserving of you. I love you, Dove. Please believe me." By the time Wes finished talking, he was at her side, his hands on her shoulders. She hesitated, wavering between pulling away from him and moving to him. Wes kept silent, knowing there was nothing more to say.

"I gave you everything," Dove whispered, another tear falling. Wes brushed it away with his thumb, cupping her cheek in his hand.

"I know," Wes replied. She bit her lip and looked up at him, blue eyes deep and sad and confused. "I never wanted to hurt you. I love you."

Dove let out a shuddering breath and leaned her head on his chest, her hands fisting in his shirt. "I love you, too," she breathed and buried her nose in his shoulder. Wes kissed her hair and wrapped his arms around her. He met Wash's eye and smiled a silent thanks. The director held up his hands, flashing ten fingers. Ten minutes. That was his gift to them before they started filming. Classic Wash. Always on a schedule, always thinking about his craft. He was still a good man.

"It's going to be alright," Wes said, kissing Dove's hair again and breathing in her clean scent. She nodded and he tightened his hold on her. He would never give her up again.

~

"Have you ever been to one of these before?" Rachel tugged at a strand of Dove's hair and pinned it into place. Meg leaned into a mirror to apply her eyeliner and snorted in derision.

"A movie premier? Are you joking? I'm a single mother who runs Dove's cafe while she becomes famous. I've never worn a formal dress before." Meg straightened and smoothed a hand over her green sheath dress, taking a deep breath and letting it out before turning to where Rachel was finishing Dove's hair. "What do you think?"

"You look lovely," Dove smiled. Meg beamed. Timmy was sleeping over at a friend's house and Rachel had come to help Dove and Meg prepare for the premier. Dove found that doing her own makeup after having someone do it for her for almost nine months was daunting, so she had accepted Rachel's help gratefully. That offer turned into an excursion for a dress and a day at the spa which Meg and Dove enjoyed thoroughly. Rachel was continuously surprised by the things neither woman had never done.

"And that's you all sorted," Rachel said, patting

Dove's shoulder. She stood from her chair and walked to the mirror, looking back at her reflection in shock. She wore a blue dress that looked like something out of an old Hollywood glamour film. The things she had worn in the film were nowhere near as grand as this and she found herself blushing at the pleasure she felt.

"Thank you," Dove turned to Rachel and smiled. "This is wonderful."

"You deserve it, love," Rachel replied. She wore a white jumper with matching jacket, claiming that she had been to too many movie premiers to get a dress. That didn't mean she didn't look good, though. Dove figured it was the woman's charm that added to the entire thing.

The buzzer sounded, making all three women jump. Dove laughed first, her hand splayed on her stomach to hide her nerves. "I think that's the driver," she said, moving to the intercom. She nodded and signalled to the others, who gathered up their coats and purses. Meg slipped her arm through Dove's and shook her head.

"I never thought I'd get to do something like this," Meg said. "Thank you, Dove."

"You earned it," Dove returned, nodding seriously at her friend. "You did more with the cafe than I ever did. Not to mention you kept me sane throughout this entire process."

Meg tossed back her head and laughed, making the driver of the town car look at her with surprise. "I think Mr. Blackwood did that for you, Dove." Dove blushed and bit her lip to hold back a smile. Meg was right.

The three women slipped into the car and were driven to the theatre where people gathered out front. It wasn't anything like one of Charlie's bigger movies, Dove later discovered, but there were still enough people to constitute a crowd and cameras were flashing as people arrived. Dove was helped out of the car by the driver amidst the noise and calls of people she had never met, but who all seemed to know who she was. Or who she pretended to be: Felicia Teague.

"Felicia! Over here," one middle-aged man with a camera said, smiling at her. Dove recognised him as one of the reporters from the first, and other, press conferences Charlie had held. She smiled and waved, both sincere. She was feeling giddy with happiness and she had no idea where it was coming from.

Normally, she hated crowds. They brought out panic in her faster than anything but being alone with a strange man. The noise was often overwhelming and she would get as far away as quickly as possible. Tonight, though, it was as though she were floating. Nothing could bother her and her eyes fairly shone with pleasure. Still, Dove moved through the crowd swiftly, mostly in part to Meg tugging on her arm to get them through the doors as quickly as possible.

"There you are." Wes' deep voice made Dove turn and she strode to him as quickly as her shoes would allow. He laughed and wrapped his arms around her waist before kissing her soundly. "I was beginning to think you changed your mind."

"I don't think Meg would have let me." Dove nodded her head towards her friend, who was looking around the decorated theatre in awe. Rachel had gone off to talk with someone she obviously knew. Charlie and Marc were standing off to one side, going over notes, of all things. Roman had just walked in the door and sauntered over to Wes and Dove.

"Quite the party, wouldn't you say?" he asked. "I wouldn't have expected as much from a romance."

"When Wash does things, he likes to do them big," Wes agreed. "Marc has already told me that there's to be an after party at the Waldorf. The first round is on Wash."

"I never thought I'd hear those words," Roman chuckled. Meg stepped up to Dove's shoulder and Roman noticed the movement almost immediately. "I don't believe we've been introduced. I'm Roman Dawes, the real star of this movie."

"Ah, I'm Meg. Dove's flatmate and business manager," Meg held out her hand for a handshake. Roman kissed the flesh lightly, making Meg blink in surprise. She looked at Dove for explanation and Dove merely laughed.

"He can be a bit forward, but he's harmless. Mostly," she said. Roman grinned and nodded, before leading Meg off to be introduced to the others. Wes tightened his hold around Dove's waist.

"Did you ever think we would get this far?" he asked quietly.

"I never thought I'd be in this situation at all," Dove said. "I thought I would be in that cafe, thinking about travelling the world."

"Speaking of travel," Wes reached into his jacket and pulled out two slips of paper, which he handed to Dove. She read them and raised her eyebrows in shock.

"The Virgin Islands?" she asked. Wes chuckled and kissed her once, just to be sure, before he pulled out something else from a pocket and set it in Dove's hand. She stared at the black velvet box, words caught in her throat and her heart shining.

"I hear they're perfect for destination weddings."

in.

ACKNOWLEDGMENTS

I should, as always, like to thank my family who supports me in all that I do. I would also like to thank Fay Lane for doing such beautiful covers; it never ceases to amaze me. And, perhaps most importantly, all my lovely readers. You put such a smile on my face!

ABOUT THE AUTHOR

Evelyn Grimald has been writing since she was a girl. When she wasn't reading, she was going about inventing stories to keep her entertained at social events like parties and dinners. Since then, she has pretended to be a touch practical and went to university, where she got degrees in linguistics. As it turns out, practicality proved to be a useful thing and now Evelyn applies her knowledge of language to writing stories.

Evelyn lives a quiet life reading and writing, which her cat and dog both appreciate. When not writing, she is walking, sewing, or reading, exploring so many of the worlds which books provide.

ALSO BY EVELYN GRIMALD

The Houndskeeper

The Wooden Rose

The Search for Reality